HAPPIER AS
WEREWOLVES

For Stefan,

If you watch "Jaws"
backwards, it's a
about a shark that
vomits up people
until they're forced to
open a beach.

ANDREW
HEATON

HAPPIER AS WEREWOLVES

A COMEDY

Andrew Heaton

Published in the United States by Last House Standing.

ISBN-13: 978-0-9896131-5-6

For Adam,

Who I would be friends with
even if we weren't brothers

And also to the many animals which Adam has befriended and/or eaten

Preface

This book was supposed to be a memoir about finding Bigfoot.

I know. I *know*.

Listen, when you're fresh out of college you do stupid things, like hunt for fabled apes, or attend law school. A lot of my friends went to law school. I went the Bigfoot route. As with many epic journeys I wound up discovering something more interesting than the original focus of my adventure. Which is *not* something you hear from my attorney friends.

None of those guys ever say, "You know, I started out studying patent law, but then I stumbled upon some mythical creatures and later they tried to eat me." So who's to judge me for combing the backwoods of my home state for half a year, prowling around for Bigfoot? At least I didn't incur debt.

A lot of my lawyer buddies fell in love in law school. With other law school students. They now own large homes in Mesta Park and Nichols Hills, with hardwood floors and neighbors who own polo shirts.

Well I fell in love, too.

Will you ever see any of this, Natalie? It's too much to hope that you'll read my account of our autumn together and forget the bad things that happened. But maybe you will at least understand why I did what I did.

Saul Heinrich

Chapter 1

You never really think about landmines until you nearly trip one with your pants down. In this case, a homespun grenade of three shotgun shells duct-taped together like a bundle of angry turnips. The backwoods munitions hobbyist had also glued carpet tacks to the outside of the wad, which in the moonlight gleamed like the Devil's hair plugs.

I took in a long, deep breath and slowly pealed my foot back from the tripwire with such focus and precision that I might as well have been performing brain surgery with my ankle. I zipped my fly and wobbled back a couple of steps, eyes still locked on the prickly do-it-yourself shrapnel. Then I dashed to my Volvo, slammed the door shut and gunned the ignition. I glanced in the rear-view mirror before lurching onto the highway, half expecting to see a deranged gun-toting local nuzzle my bumper with his pickup.

I was in banjo territory. The lethal kind.

I made a mental note to mention the incident to Cindy when I arrived in Hugo, a small outpost in the southern-flavored patch of Oklahoma known as Little Dixie. She had explicitly warned me about clandestine cannabis plantations, but I had dismissed her advice as Reader's Digest paranoia. The idea that a state with more cows than people could also hold within its borders a Hee-Haw Vietnam of explosives, shotguns, and a thriving marijuana industry struck me as ludicrous. Of course, that was before a urinary pit stop delivered me to a garden noir, nearly blowing my gonads off in a demon's sneeze of carpet tacks and buckshot.

I still desperately needed to use the bathroom, but decided to press on to the next town, where fear of death could be swapped for more manageable concerns about gas station hygiene.

Fortunately, I reached a little speedtrap in short order, nestled in the rolling nubs of the Kiamichis. Small enough it could have posted "Welcome to" and "You're leaving" on the same pole. Not that it had a sign. No markers at all. Just a sleepy, unmarked hamlet anonymously straddling the road, poking out of the forest like the ominous beginnings of a bald spot. It would take another four months before I realized why the town failed to announce itself to passing motorists, or why the state map conveniently forgot to mention it.

The town's single gas station was a slumping convenience store with elderly pumps and no allegiance to any petroleum chain I recognized. I hobbled out of my car and up to the station's door, only to see the baby blue "We're Open" sign flip over to its red and black "Sorry, We're Closed" alter ego. Inside, the innards of the gas station were visible from the windows in fluorescent clarity. Three codgers in triplet John Deer hats sat hunched over coffee mugs at a linoleum counter. Behind them, a scrawny kid, probably nicknamed "Squirt" or "Junior," fiddled with a cash register. The scene

2

looked like the rural version of an Edward Hopper painting.

I ignored the "Sorry, We're Closed" sign and pushed the door open anyway. The largest coffee-swiller leaped from his seat to block me. "We're closed."

"It's only eight o'clock," I said. "I just need to use the bathroom. I'll—"

"You have a good evening, then." He shut the glass door and locked it before returning to his companions. They cast icy stares in my direction until I finally waddled back to the car, my engorged bladder violently demanding release.

I slumped into the seat and groaned. I rolled down my window and flipped them the bird as I drove away. The gesture seemed to perk the geezers up. They all grinned and displayed their own middle fingers, as if they hadn't had an opportunity for blatant rudeness in years and found the experience exhilarating. The kid behind the counter waved, oblivious.

I decided to pull over as quickly as possible to relieve myself, then swore when I realized I had parked in front of a cemetery. I couldn't take a leak in a graveyard. Not because of any particular religious convictions. Just basic decorum. Plus, a month earlier one of my frat brothers had been arrested for pissing within spitting distance of a playground around midnight while drunk one evening, and now he's on the sex offender registry. So I couldn't quite bring myself to tinkle with reckless abandon, even in the middle of nowhere.

I staggered away from the consecrated ground of the local necropolis towards the nearest tree and unzipped my pants. I let go and moaned with relief, rolling my eyes as I rocked back and forth like a sprinkler. Then something caught my attention. Glossier tombstones nearby reflected the town's pumpkin-colored lights, but the glistening slabs each blinked, one by one. Someone obscured their reflections as they came towards me. Me, the guy with his pants around his ankles, his family jewels exposed to the wind and whatever lunatic cowboys hang out in boneyards after hours.

"C'mon, c'mon," I urged, gritting my teeth as my internal hydraulic pressure increased to the point of potentially creating diamonds.

A pair of glowing green eyes materialized and shimmered in the Volvo's headlights. I yelped and bolted, tripping over my pants, then scurried to the car with my underwear around my knees. I slammed the door shut behind me, a fraction of a second before something thumped against it. I looked down from the window and saw a coyote peering up at me, teeth bared. I screamed and hit the accelerator, fishtailing through the grass before lurching onto the road and over a second coyote.

There are few sounds in life less pleasant than that of a large animal executing a death-roll beneath the undercarriage of your car. On what turned out to be my worst Valentine's Day date ever, I once throttled an indecisive squirrel. It made a *thwippit* noise which suddenly pushed my date out of her budding libido and into what ultimately became a long, successful career as a lesbian. But that horrid squeal was nothing compared to the yelp and sinister twirl of coyote limbs cracking against the underbelly of my Volvo.

I slammed on the brakes and gripped the wheel, breathing hard and sweating. Why did I leave the car? I don't know. There are times when I wonder if I am anything more than an assortment of hormone-squirting valves and credit card debt. Guilt is only one of a startling array of motivators which compels me to do stupid things. So I hopped out of the car with an aim of cradling the bleeding coyote, having entirely forgot about the other animal still prowling the area.

I cinched my pants up, took a step, then froze solid as an ominous howl rose from the woods. And another. And still more. An honor guard of hulking canine beasts which bore scant resemblance to their scrawny cousins you sometimes see scavenging in fields. I heard dozens of them all raising their snouts in a monstrous funeral dirge, baying at the moon— and at me. I tiptoed back to my car, quietly shut the door, then locked it. Something ran past my tail lights, and I saw a huge coyote sniff the bleeding sprawl of its friend. It looked directly into my rear view mirror, then growled. I could hear the rumble of its throat through the glass.

That was enough for me. I put the car in drive and puttered away. Feeling a little spooked, I turned the radio on as I cruised out of the eldritch town. Creedence Clearwater Revival's "Bad Moon Rising" filled the car.

I am not a religious man. But I *am* superstitious. Whatever forces bind this world we live in were toying with me through the airwaves. At the time I thought nothing of it. Now I know it wasn't a coincidence. It was an omen.

Chapter 2

"And there ran mute behind him such a hound of hell as God forbid should ever be at my heels."

—Sir Arthur Conan Doyle
The Hound of the Baskervilles

I used to be in love with Cindy. Or thought I was, anyway. It might be more accurate to say that I desperately wanted to have sex with Cindy, and also, simultaneously, liked her as a friend. So I thought I was in love with her.

As a sophomore in college I couldn't tell the difference between these two states. The concept of an appealing yet platonic friend hadn't yet entered my realm of consciousness, but fortunately she suffered from no romantic illusions regarding our friendship. She adroitly navigated around the moguls of awkwardness I dumped into conversations, until my madness passed and we settled into a fulfilling friendship.

She sat at her parents' house, cross-legged in an inflatable lounge chair, one of several pieces of dormitory flotsam and jetsam which had accompanied her back to her home town of Hugo after graduation. Technicolor wind chimes she made herself dangled from each ear lobe, and a chain of half-melted belt buckles draped off her collar bones. All baubles from her workshop.

On this particular evening, the first time I had

seen her since graduation, she looked especially impish.

"So how was the drive?" she asked.

"Pretty good. Little to no traffic to speak of. I listened to some music, made pretty good time. Oh — and I almost blew my leg to pieces by tripping some bumpkin's landmine tripwire."

"What kind of music did you listen to?"

"Whatever came over the radio. Did you hear the bit about landmines?"

She shrugged. "I *told* you to be careful around here. Stick to main roads, don't go off exploring."

"Well, that's going to be problematic," I said. "Since for the next few weeks I'll be exploring a lot."

She shrugged and took another sip of beer. "Maybe you should explore someplace else, that hasn't been explored. This place has maps and everything. You'd be a little redundant."

"I'm looking for something in particular," I said. "And I've seen your so-called 'maps' and they're ridiculous."

"Like what?"

"I drove through an entire town that wasn't on the map. How do you forget to label a town?"

"So," Cindy said, stroking an invisible beard, "either the map company is full of idiots or you, who don't know the area, made a wrong turn and misidentified where you are. This is a tough one!"

"I *did* know where I was. It's across the hills from Nambersaw."

Cindy cocked her head and squinted, deep in thought. "Could be Lycan. I think they have a watermelon festival coming up."

I almost asked her about the queer coyote

incident, but she steered the conversation in a new direction. "What are you looking for down here anyway. Treasure?"

"Bigfoot hunting," I said, in the same matter-of-fact tone you would use to describe a prostate exam. When my grant initially came through I was elated, but became slightly more embarrassed each time I had to explain my quest to find the undiscovered North American primate.

"Uh-huh," she said skeptically, "In southeast Oklahoma. Of course. I thought Bigfoot was more of a West Coast thing. Also imaginary."

"The Pacific Northwest is a lot larger and has more documented encounters, but there are still a number of reports trickling in from around here. Mountains and forests make for good ape men hideouts."

"Do you think you'll find him?" she asked. "We could put an ad in the local paper. Maybe he'll check it out, meet you for coffee or something."

"You just keep laughing it up until I win the Nobel Prize."

She finished her beer and set it gingerly on a nearby coaster. "So will you be living in the woods for three months?"

"Mostly," I said. "My grandfather lives in Nambersaw, and his property backs right up to the Kiamichi mountains. So I'll use his house as a base camp, but spend a lot of time on woodland excursions."

"Your grandfather?" she asked. "Is this Grampa Rabbi?" Her balloonish recliner squeaked as she sat upright. "Can I meet him? I've never met a rabbi."

"He's *not* a rabbi," I said, conveying through the

8

pitch of my voice just how many times I had corrected this mistake.

Cindy bolted out of her chair, already excited about her next idea. "I made you something!" She gestured for me to follow her out the back door.

Her sprawl of art projects looked like an airplane crash in the backyard. Dozens of half-melted, spider-like sculptures sprouted from the lawn. Insects welded together from fenders and mufflers. In between these stretched the silhouettes of robots; clunky 1930's creations frozen in the positions of Olympic athletes. Paint can totem poles dotted the fence.

She opened the door to the tool shed and flipped a swinging yellow bulb on. Half-assembled robot parts littered the interior. In the center of the room a robot skeleton, welded together from crowbars, drill bits and ball bearings, sat ponderously in a reproduction of Rodan's *The Thinker*.

Cindy loved robots. This single bridge into science fiction is what paved the way for our friendship. Even today, whenever Cindy gets depressed about something, she makes a robot costume for herself out of cardboard boxes and spray paint, then sits around her apartment watching chick flicks and drinking mojitos.

"You made me a sculpture?" I asked, enthralled. It would take some serious Tetris skills to load one into the Volvo, but I had always secretly coveted Cindy's crazy automaton statues.

"No," she corrected. She floated between her two work benches, lightly brushing tools with the tips of her fingers. She unclenched the vice at the end of the table and withdrew a silver ring. "Here!" she said, shoving it towards my face. I plucked it from her. She stood arms akimbo in anticipation of praise.

"It's lovely," I commented, observing the smooth surface of the ring. A silver band with a groove on either edge.

"Flip it over!" She put her fists up to her mouth as if to keep the excitement from escaping her body.

A Star of David winked at me. Each blue line composing it disappeared under the next, as if part of a wreath. "It's wonderful," I said, trying to hide the misgivings in my voice. The quality of the piece was staggering. How on earth had she crafted the tiny embossed lines of the star? They sat slightly higher than the silver background, in perfect placement. I take items of craftsmanship for granted, assuming they originate in some soulless Beijing factory. But looking down at the ring, I had no idea how Cindy could bang out such a trinket. "Amazing. How on earth do you do this?"

Cindy frowned. "You don't like it?"

"No, no, I *do.*"

"I kind of thought you would be more excited." She sounded irritated, edging towards passive-aggressive.

"I *am* excited." I slid it onto my right hand.

"Okay," she said, although we could both tell the moment fell short of her expectations. The incident made me glad we were only friends, because she could slather silent tension onto a situation like tar.

"It's just," I said, then stopped.

"What?"

"I'm not *exactly* Jewish." Our family is a proud clan of fake Jews, stretching all the way back to

Grampa.

*

The next morning we woke up early to see the circus animals. When the circus shuts down for winter after touring the country, the animals stay in Hugo. For years the circus employed her father as a part-time pachyderm maintenance hand. During the warmer months he ran a private taxidermy business in town, but when the circus returned each year in September to hibernate his career shifted to the daily chores of feeding elephants and camels and later shoveling their droppings.

It was now September. Summer had finally succumbed to death after a valiant fight, and early mornings were marked by a pleasant chill and the ghostly breath of condensation. We stood outside the hangar-like barns with her dad, who systematically unbolted locks. He had a hulking torso, with forearms so imposing it seemed someone had lodged grapefruits inside of his tendons.

"There sure are a bunch of locks," I said, keeping up the same quality of repertoire which marked my relationship with Leonard.

"There used to be less," he said, jiggling a knee-level bolt, "but six years ago a couple of high schoolers got drunk, broke in, and released some of the animals." I laughed, but stopped abruptly when he stood up to lock his frozen eye-balls with mine. "We're lucky no one got hurt from that, Saul. Can you imagine what would have happened if someone hit an elephant at high-speed?"

"Wouldn't someone *see* an elephant coming?" I

ventured.

Leonard did not respond. For some reason, Cindy's father had suffered under the same delusion I once did, that I would end up marrying his daughter. Eventually it became obvious to all parties involved that this was not the case, and my continued presence in her life confused and irritated the man. Despite no official romance with Cindy, Leonard viewed me as her ex-boyfriend and dealt with me with all the according stiff awkwardness.

We entered the barn and relaxed in the immediate comfort of animal body heat. It reeked of hay, feed and manure, yet somehow felt familiar and comforting in this regard. Green light filtered onto the straw from the colored Plexiglas in the ceiling. "Grab a bucket of elephant chow," he ordered. Cindy and I giggled at the phrase "elephant chow," but halted when Leonard turned to stare at me. "Over there." He motioned to a wall with stacks of buckets.

"Peanuts?" I asked.

He sighed, as if such a question bled energy from his soul. "Saul, do you have any idea how many peanuts an animal the size of an elephant would have to consume?"

I shrugged. "I'm guessing it's about the same in volume as the elephant chow we're going to feed them." Cindy and I grabbed a bucket and caught up with him.

Leonard pointed to each separate pachyderm as he pronounced their names. "Dole, Newt, Strom, Rush—"

"Newt?" I asked, suppressing a laugh. "Is he the runt of the litter, or what?"

Leonard shook his head. "All of the elephants

are named after famous Republicans. Their stage names are different."

"Why would a circus elephant need a stage name?" Cindy asked. "It's not like they have to conceal their identities from other elephants, is it?"

Leonard dumped the bucket of pellets into a trough. "I just feed them, sweetie. Feed them and scoop up their shit."

She drifted among the various mammals, alternatively stroking camels, elephants and donkeys. "Daddy, can I pet the tiger?"

"No!"

Although Cindy never said so, I imagine the circus animals were half the reason she returned home after college. Her fiancée broke up with her the night after graduation, then signed up for the Peace Corps and disappeared. Cindy never forgave him for that—abandoning her for well-digging in Rwanda, thereby depriving her of the fiery hatred she needed for the breakup process. Dumbstruck by the sudden sharp-right her future had made, she retreated to her parent's home in Hugo to assist her father in circus animal care and to create a whole gallery's worth of robot sculptures and jewelry.

At noon we broke for lunch. Leonard elected to hollow out a sack lunch alone, while Cindy and I scuttled to a dubious fast food joint called Barney's Burger Basement, all of which stood above ground.

"Do you think your father fantasizes about stuffing the elephants?" I asked.

Cindy nodded. "How could you *not*?" She finished the last of her root beer through a straw, then continued sucking until no possible moisture could be hiding beneath the ice. "I mean, c'mon, an

13

elephant? A lion? He probably took the job thinking they would give him a body if one ever keeled over."

"Then what?" I asked. "What would he do with a gigantic stuffed mammal?"

Cindy thought hard about this. "I suppose he would build a new wing of the house to keep it in. Or sell it, I guess." She crumpled her foil hamburger wrapper and tossed it into the back of my car. "If you should inadvertently hit a sasquatch with your car, I bet Dad would stuff it for you, free of charge."

"Good to know," I said, gulping down the last of my greasy burger.

"Do you think you'll find one?" she asked.

"Jane Goodall thinks there's an undiscovered North American primate."

"If Jane Goodall believed in leprechauns, would you go looking for them?"

"Yes," I sneered. "A pot of gold is a way better prize than a bleeding hairy ape carcass."

"So you plan to shoot him?"

I crumpled my foil wrapper. "Of course not. I doubt I'll even see him. We're talking about a hominid who's smart enough to evade any researchers who've ever looked for one."

Cindy leaned back and put her legs on the dashboard. "Then why bother? Why spend three months poking around the woods by yourself?"

"Ah, see, I'm *not* by myself. The way I pitched the project to Wily College is more as an anthropological survey of people who *think* they've seen a sasquatch than actually finding one. Regardless of whether I get a hair sample or some plaster foot prints, I'll be able to collect stories about Bigfoot sightings." I leaned into the backseat of the

14

Volvo and fished out a notebook. "We'll start with you. Ever seen Bigfoot?"

"No," Cindy said, admiring herself in a mirror. "Boy, you suck at Bigfoot research."

"Do you know anyone who has seen Bigfoot?"

She turned to face me. "Yes, actually." I raised my eyebrows. "Except around here they don't call it Bigfoot, they call it the Green Hills Monster. Dad saw it as a kid once. He said it stood six feet tall and smelled *horrible*."

"Your dad?" I asked, scribbling his name down.

"Yes, but don't ask him about it. He would never tell anyone, and he'd get mad at me for mentioning it at all."

"Okay."

"Some kids in my high school class said they saw it once." She dropped her feet from the dashboard. "Four or five guys, they all still live around here. I can give you their names if you'd like."

"Yeah," I said, handing her the notebook. "What happened?"

"According to them," she said, speaking slowly as she jotted names down, "they were out in the woods one night and heard a lot of weird noises. Sticks banging together, then some crashing from the woods. Something charged them, and they ran back to their cars and drove off."

"A lot of people report hearing sticks bang together," I said. "I think it might be some kind of auditory territory marker for bigfoots."

She handed the notebook to me and slid the pen behind my ear. "When they came back the next day one of their cars was missing its front bumper. They

15

found it wrapped around a tree trunk."

"*Really?*" I asked. Good stuff.

"Yeah," she said, getting bored with the conversation. "There was a picture in the paper or something, I forget. I bet one of them cut the article out."

"Wow. Yeah, that's helpful. Thanks."

"Hey listen," she said, turning to look at me. "*I* don't think there's a Green Hills Monster. I grew up here, and it seems a lot more likely that the Green Hills Monster only turns up when people are drunk or stoned. The boys I know probably got schnockered and hit a tree with their car, then made up the whole story to keep their parents from killing them."

"What about your dad?"

She smiled. "I guess by my logic he must have been drunk, right? Or, I think, he was probably just a kid with an overactive imagination." She leaned over and turned the ignition for me. "I dunno. Let's go feed the lions!"

*

That evening I maneuvered my Volvo around the Kiamichi Mountains, which was not terribly difficult as they would otherwise be called "hills" in any state with a view of snowy peaks. The Kiamichis are not staggering, but they are pretty, and I enjoyed driving through them. I grew up in a flat town called Hoople and consequently picture my homeland as a vast pancake slathered with wheat and pockets of cattle. The southeastern quadrant of the state, littered with hills and forests, shadows and trees, always filled me with unexpected pride. Like discovering that your otherwise banal, milquetoast parents secretly indulge in falconry on weekends.

I skirted a bend and hit my brakes as a town leaped out from nowhere. My car shuddered as I matched my deceleration with the rapid fire of speed zone postings designed to all but halt traffic, milking tickets from the non-compliant. It took only a moment to recognize the anonymous village as the site of the previous evening's coyote massacre, what Cindy said might be Lycan. Same pumpkin-colored streetlights, same leaning water tower shaped like a radio antenna with an egg jammed on top.

I passed the cemetery and slowed as I noticed people. Seven of them. Huddled together in the darkness, posted around an eager new tombstone and a fresh pile of earth. My lights washed over the assembly and I caught sight of their attire. Everyone wore black, the women in church hats and the men in suits. Their briefly illumined, somber faces turned to stare at the rubbernecking Volvo as I sputtered past. Their eyes reflected off the headlights like silver dollars.

"A *funeral?*" I asked aloud. "At nine-thirty at night?" I jumped slightly as a streak of fur dashed past my car. In the rear view mirror three coyotes collected in the middle of the road, fixated on my disappearing Volvo.

Weird.

I drove off, out of the unmapped hamlet and onto the highway.

Who has a funeral at night?

Chapter 3

"But Peter paid no attention to his grandfather's words. Boys like Peter aren't afraid of wolves."

—Sergei Prokofiev, *Peter and the Wolf*

I decided to spend my first night of the grant camping, preferring my own company to that of my huckster grandfather. Although, I severely miscalculated my own boredom threshold when sober and camping by myself. While I had plenty of paperbacks in my trunk, I didn't want to squander my flashlight batteries and I hadn't brought a CD player. After a hardy dinner of baked beans followed by a hero's portion of s'mores, I finally fished my cell phone out and checked the reception.

Two bars. Not a lot, but enough. I dialed Cindy.

"Hey, mister!" she said. "Did you find Bigfoot?"

"No. I spent most of the day searching for tracks, but none belonged to gigantic apes."

"Aww, well don't beat yourself up. Rome didn't find Bigfoot in a day."

"Right. What are you up to?" Metal clinked together from the other side of the receiver. "Artsy robot construction?"

"You know it," said Cindy, "There's an art festival in Austin this November and I'm making calls to see if I can enter. My collection is called *Pygmalion's Aluminum.* I'm four robots shy of completion."

"Still working on *The Thinker*?"

"No, he's finished. Now I'm building a gumball machine robot styled after Munch's *The Scream*. I call it, *C: Drive not found*."

"Brilliant."

"And what are you doing?"

"Camping. I'm perched on a log about ten minutes from Grampa's house. Tomorrow I'll move further north, then the next day into the Quachitas."

"Is it pretty?"

"Yes," I said, but—" I stopped. I thought I saw something move through the trees.

"But what?" asked Cindy.

"Hold on," I whispered. I strained to look past the campfire, into the forest, searching for movement. Nothing. "Sorry," I said, my voice back to normal. "I thought I saw something."

"Don't scare me!" Cindy said, playful.

"Why would *you* be scared?" I asked. "I'm the one perched on a log in the woods. All you have to worry about is robot art gone awry. Did—" I froze. A figure. The silent outline of a person, illuminated for a split second as it stepped from behind one tree to another.

"Cindy?" I whispered. "I think someone's out here."

"Stop!" she pleaded.

"I'm serious."

"Call the police!" she demanded, scared and angry because of it.

"No, not yet." I stared into the sleeping scrub oaks. A chill played the xylophone up and down my spinal column. A human seemed much more frightening in this environment than a cougar.

Because, I thought, why wouldn't a human announce himself?

"Saul?" Cindy asked, beginning to panic. "This isn't funny."

"I'm sorry." My voice returned to normal. I forced myself to speak in an even, steady tone. "I know I've only been out here for a night, but being alone in the woods plays tricks on your mind." And my imagination had plenty of help. After Wily College awarded me my anthropological grant to look for Bigfoot, I had written Grampa to let him know he'd see me over the summer, and his response had been a brief congratulations with a stern admonishment that the forest behind his house was a breeding ground for rabid mountain lions and homicidal lunatics. I took that to mean he was looking forward to our reunion about as much as I was.

"I'm just seeing things," I assured myself by telling Cindy. "Don't worry."

"I *am* worried, asshole." She clinked a wrench against something metal to punctuate her sentiment. "Don't play with me just because you're bored."

"I'm not." I took a deep breath. "Actually, this is exactly what I wrote my senior thesis about. 'Paranoid Apes,' by Solomon Heinrich."

"The culmination of your college experience was an essay about suspicious monkeys?"

"Well... yes," I admitted. "The theory is this: we're descended from hunter-gatherers, who are descended from various stages of hominids and apes."

"I've actually heard this theory before."

"Let me finish. Let's say that you and I are our

hominid ancestors, living twenty million years ago in the Serengeti."

"Okay."

"We're both sitting around a campfire, just like I am now. Except that *I'm* a nervous, paranoid hominid, whereas you're calm and emotionally balanced."

"I'm the psychologically stable monkey."

"Yes," I said, "and that's exactly why you die."

"What?"

"You get devoured for that exact reason. Because," I continued, "night after night *I* sleep lightly. While we sit around our campfire grunting, I keep *thinking* I detect predators in the bush. I'm on alert."

"But they aren't really there?"

"Most of the time, no. Ninety percent of the time I'm only imagining something. But on that rare occasion where my paranoia coincides with a sneak saber tooth attack, *I'm* prepared. You, the stable, reasonable hominid have nodded off. And you are devoured."

"So," Cindy said, putting it together, "our species is descended from paranoid monkeys."

"Exactly. Only edgy hominids survived long enough to reproduce. The significance is that their descendants, us, have brains wired to seek out danger and intelligence. As I'm sitting here at this campfire, my brain is constantly *looking* for eyes, movement, threats. Left to its own, it will imagine things. Mild, protective hallucination."

"That's fascinating."

"The conclusion," I said, "is that it accounts for most paranormal encounters. It's not that people are making up ghosts, or even that they're crazy. It's that their minds are hyper-sensitive to anything which might be construed as intelligence. It's like a hair-trigger car alarm."

"So you think that's where ghosts stories and Bigfoot come from?"

"Mostly," I admitted. "There are occasional instances which can't be written off. But yes, most of the time I think encounters with the unknown are the neurological legacy of our paranoid ape forefathers."

"I think I agree with you," reflected Cindy. In the distance a howl pierced the night. "What is *that?*"

"Sounds like a coyote," I said, as other bays joined in. "Don't worry, they're at least a mile away."

"All the same, what's your plan if a mountain lion jumps out, or Bigfoot tries to mate you?"

"A combination of head-butting and bare-handed strangling."

"Seriously."

"I always take a machete with me when I go camping. A sharp one."

"Glad to hear it. Do you mind if I let you go? I just had an idea for *C: Drive not found.*"

"Not at all," I said. "Thanks for keeping me company."

"Any time."

I flipped the phone shut and dropped it back into my pocket. In the distance, the howls reared up again, as if trying to coax the moon down for a visit. They sounded a little closer. I decided to get my machete out of the tent, just in case.

I turned around, and froze. Six feet away, directly between me and the pup tent, stood a wolf.

My body locked, rigid in an otherwise casual

position on the log. It had to be a wolf. Coyotes are gangly creatures. They look like emaciated, dirt-colored huskies. The creature between me and my machete was the size of a Great Dane. Well fed, with a cinnamon-colored coat. It looked like a fox and Husky had made a baby on steroids.

Just sitting there. It's eyes gleaming like lanterns from the campfire behind me.

It stared at me intently but calmly. I fought the urge to bolt. How long had the wolf been watching? Did Oklahoma even *have* wolves? And weren't they supposed to be afraid of people?

Not this one. It had sneaked up, sat around, listened to the human babble of my phone call. I decided the best idea was to keep the status quo. Play it cool. Maybe the wolf *was* just a Husky. Yes, that made much more sense. That would explain why it came up to me in the first place—a domesticated breed, even in the wild, would still have a basic camp follower instinct.

"Hello, fella," I said in my calmest, most soothing, most absolutely we-are-all-mellow-friends-here voice.

It stood up. And snarled.

I glanced behind me at the fire. The last log I deposited on the embers had finally combusted at the end. If I could grab it, I might be able to scare the wild dog away.

The animal looked at the fire, *at the log*, then turned to me. The hackles on its back rose in angry chains of muscle that twitched beneath its fur. "Easy, easy," I soothed. It let out a low, terrible growl, as if a marble-sized chunk of thunder were giving it indigestion.

I stepped toward the fire and it lunged, snapping at me. Instinctively, I jumped away, and suddenly found the wolf blocking me from any sort of weapon. It did not repeat the lunge. Instead, it took a step towards me. I took a step back.

It took another.

I did the same.

And so it went for ten minutes. The wolf growling, head lowered and ears flattened, pacing toward me. Each time it approached I retreated, keeping the same pace. My head pounded. Sweat dripped from my body. I wanted to turn and run, but knew if I did that some primordial chase instinct in the wolf would snap, and I would feel the lacerations of gleaming incisors.

We continued the dance of death for fifteen minutes, step by step. Limbs scraped my back and cut against my cheeks. What would happen when I finally tripped? Surely the sudden movement would undo me. The wolf would lunge, and that would be that. It would tear my jugular open like a ketchup packet.

I could barely push through the trees. A branch jammed into my kidney and snapped. The forest became so dark I could hardly see the wolf at all. Only the reflection of the moon in its horrible yellow eyes, and the steady crunch of leaves beneath it.

Then the maze of limbs gave way to naked stars, and my feet rustled against grass. I darted my head to the side and saw rows of grapes. When I turned back to the wolf, it snarled. The hackles on its back seemed to sprout more hackles, as if the creature's muscles were reproducing beneath its hide. I took another step back, and fell.

The wolf didn't kill me. I sat up on my elbows and it snapped at me, nearly biting my knee. I half-screamed, and it pulled back a step, getting ready to pounce. Then, when I thought everything was about to end in a fountain of blood and a tangle of fur, the wolf retreated to the edge of the trees. Maintaining eye contact, it lifted its leg and urinated. It tilted its head back and howled, making my body involuntarily shudder. Then, in a flash, it disappeared into the forest.

I bolted through the familiar vineyards of my grandfather's property and up to his house. "Grampa! GRAMPA!" I yelled, ponding at the door. "There's a—"

The door flung open and the business end of a shotgun tapped my forehead. "Saul?" he asked. "That you?"

"Yes!" I batted the gun away and glowered at him. "I just nearly got mauled in the woods!"

"No," Grampa said, clicking the safety button on the gun, "you just nearly bought yourself a discount haircut, courtesy of Remington Outdoor Company. You should be damned happy arthritis has slowed my trigger finger, bucko. Come on, get in." He shut the door behind me and locked it. "Now would you like to explain why the hell you're pounding at my door at," he checked his watch, "*ten* o'clock at night?"

"A wolf," I said.

His eyebrows peaked. "Indeed?" He slung the shotgun underneath his arm and nodded. "Well," he said, in a thick, twangy drawl, "I wrote you to mind the predators, didn't I?"

"You told me there are *mountain* lions," I

seethed. "Not fucking *timber* wolves!"

He smiled and walked towards his bedroom. "I didn't think you would believe me about the wolves." He gestured absently behind him to the stairs. "Make yourself at home, but don't make a mess." He flipped off the lights to the hall and shut the door behind him.

Chapter 4

"The boy cried 'Wolf, wolf!' and the villagers came out to help him."

– Aesop

The smell of bacon and coffee roused me from sleep. I swung my legs over the bed and squinted at my watch. 8:30. From the window I could see pickups already collecting on the front lawn. I slid into a pair of blue jeans and a button-up shirt and walked to the kitchen. My relative was nowhere in sight, but had left a plate of nutritious *traif* for me on the table. Bacon, eggs, half a sausage and a note:

"Saul—be happy that overgrown terrier scared you back to the house. Because guess what? Today is Rosh Hashanah! Come outside when you've eaten, I can use an extra hand. —GR"

I grunted, dropped a rock of fused cane sugar granules into a cup of coffee, and stepped out of the house.

Grampa could not have picked a finer day for the grape stomp. Billowing islands of clouds lumbered across the sky, but without any of the foreboding gray of thunderheads. Sunlight fell in soft beams across the twenty acres of grape vines, upgrading the air from "chilly" to "crisp."

Six large, Dutch-style windmills strategically guarded the vineyard; rickety old contraptions capable of sending Don Quixote into hysterics. Snow

27

and frost aren't problematic during winter because the vines are dormant, but if a sudden cold snap should descend in the spring it can kill the vines' infantile flowers and abort an entire season of crops. As this kind of hazard results primarily from air frost, Grampa erected the windmills in the late eighties to break up the draft, or keep the flow moving, or something. I confess I don't know the mechanics of it.

In any case, the combination of slowly pivoting windmills, orderly rows of vines and the wooded gums of the Kiamichi Mountains behind them looked stunning. Had Grampa ever opened up a bed and breakfast, it would have grossed as least as much as his wine. The vineyard was a Bordeaux embassy dropped into Little Dixie, and I could sense the self-respect it cultivated in the attending guests. Parents dressed in plaid and jean jackets stood around sipping coffee, talking in the calm hush proper to morning. Their children ran amok up and down the rows of vines, swinging baskets in clumsy loops, occasionally head-butting one another and shattering the morning's peace with shrieks.

Grampa sat holding court at one of the assembled picnic tables scattered between the house and grapes. His puffy white beard contrasted with his black suit and black Stetson cowboy hat. A Hasidic wrangler in rattlesnake boots. Above him hung a spray-painted banner: "Happy Rosh Hashanah!"

It wasn't. Or at least I doubt it was. I think Rosh Hashanah might actually be in September, but the shared month is all the holiday had in common with Grampa's jubilee of the same name. I sat down at the picnic table to warily observe him chat up a visitor.

"Rosh Hashanah is the Festival of Grapes," he explained. "Today Jews all around the world are harvesting the fruit of their labors. From the ancient gardens of Judea to the vineyards of the Russian steppes." He clasped his hands solemnly. "It unites our people. Through the harvest, we are all tenders of the same plot, the same vineyard." He raised his bushy eyebrows dramatically. "Earth."

His eyes twinkled. They gleefully shimmered whenever the old man lied, which is probably why no one in Nambersaw ever got around to shooting him. He swindled with such *joy*. Most folks could not help but view him as a harmless, eccentric would-be felon. Time and time again he forsook legitimate, lucrative business ventures to carry on lying to people for handfuls of pennies. And he loved it. He adored the people he stole from, and executed all his scams with the unbridled delight of a seven-year-old.

The man across from him lapped it up. Probably from Oklahoma City or Tulsa, on a day trip with his family. Most likely he had read about the Rosh Hashanah Grape Stomp in *The Gazette*. Grampa glanced down at his pocket watch. "Will you excuse me?" he asked.

He stood up from the table and cleared his throat. "Shalom!" he bellowed, letting his Ozark drawl drag out the Hebrew syllables beyond their normal scope. "It is my pleasure and honor to welcome y'all to this year's Rosh Hashanah." He slung a leathery hand against his sternum and bowed slightly. "It warms my heart to see the community celebrate this holiday with us. It is a testament to the good people of Nambersaw and

29

Little Dixie that so many gentiles want to participate in a festival beyond the scope of their own heritage. As your neighbor, I'm humbled by your love and open-mindedness." He leaned forward and winked. "Hey! You gentiles are all right!" The crowd laughed.

"Okay!" he said, wrapping it up. "Enjoy the harvest! When you're done, burgers are on me. Anyone who picks grapes gets half-off on our reserve merlot." He grabbed a coffee cup from the man speaking to him moments earlier and held it up in a toast. "L'chaim!"

"L'chaim!" the crowd returned. A few people clapped. Folks collected their baskets and wheel barrows, ambling off into the ranks of grapes.

Grampa sat down and smiled at me. I nodded. "Good morning," I said. Despite myself, the man impressed me. Over the past two decades he had built up Rosh Hashanah into a popular regional event. A pleasant, yearly festival more anticipated than the Nambersaw Chili Cookoff, but less beloved than the salvo of fireworks locals detonated when celebrating Independence Day. My grandfather's faux holiday cut the cost of harvesting grapes by a third. People did it for *free*.

Grampa returned to his seat and gestured towards me. "This is my grandson," he said, "Solomon Heinrich." His chest swelled. "He just graduated *with honors* from Wily College. Archaeology," he added.

"Anthropology," I corrected.

He snapped his fingers and pointed at me, eyes wide. "*Exactly.*"

"How did your family come to Nambersaw?" the man asked.

Grampa turned serious. "Well, we came over from Germany, actually. For various reasons." Accurate family history, in fact.

His companion nodded gravely. "Are you. . . did you get out before the Holocaust?"

The old man sat a few moments, collecting his thoughts. "My grandfather immigrated just before the turn of the century, so yes. Other members of the family," he shrugged, trailed off. "We're quite fortunate. I'll leave it at that."

I couldn't take anymore. "*Grampa,*" I said. "Our last name is *Heinrich,* for crying out loud! If we had any kin who died in concentration camps it's probably because they fell off a guard tower."

Grampa eyed me warily. "That's an old joke, Saul. And not in good taste, either." He sternly nodded toward the vineyard. "Why don't you make yourself useful and supervise the grape stomp?"

I obliged. I drifted through the rows of vines and watched children play tag until their parents trickled my way, bearing full baskets and blank expressions. "Merlot?" I asked a mustachio in a straw hat. He looked down at the tiny red grapes in his basket and shrugged. "From this row?" I asked, pointing to a particular section. He nodded. I gestured to a blue pickup parked nearby. Grampa had lined the truck bed with a plastic tarp, and a sketched "MERLOT" on a sign stretching across the rear window. Pickups for hauling the other types of grape had been parked throughout the vineyard, as if by a very careless valet.

I drifted out to the edge of the vineyard, daydreaming about my triumphant press conference after befriending a tribe of Bigfoots and returning with incontrovertible proof, but snapped out of it when I heard a scream. I looked back at the rows of grapes, expecting to see a kid clutching a snapped femur or impaled by a pitchfork, given the high-intensity of the screech. Instead I saw a chubby androgynous kid shrieking at the top of his/her lungs, clawing his/her way up one of the windmills. A wolf stood beneath him/her, wagging its tail and happily jumping up to snap at the kid's sneakers.

"Little girl!" I yelled. "Hang on! I'll go get someone!"

"I'm a *boy!*" the kid screamed. "I am *not* a girl!" He made a lunge for one of the passing spokes of the windmill and nearly fell off. "My mom cuts my hair with a bowl! It's not my fault!"

"Kid! Just *hang on*, okay? Don't grab at the windmill blades, you'll knock your head off!"

The wolf jumped up and snagged one of his shoelaces. The child screamed and clamored further up the wood, barely dislodging the tennis shoe before the animal pulled him down. Below him, the wolf flung the shoe back and forth, as if breaking the neck of a rabbit. It dropped the sneaker to the ground and lunged for the kid's toes again. "I play baseball! Do I look like a stupid girl, pee-breath? I'm a *boy!*"

"Yeah, I know!" I yelled. "You're very obviously a strapping lad, okay? Now pull your legs up and *don't* move!"

I spun around and made a dash to the house. "Wolf! Wolf!" I yelled, waving my arms frantically. I searched for Grampa but couldn't spot him. Instead I ran over to a group of men and pointed back toward the rows of grapes. "Guys! There's a wolf out there! He's treed some little fat kid with a tragic haircut!"

The men paid no attention to me. (Except for a chubby balding man who probably recognized the description of his son, but did not want to immediately own up to him.) They stared off towards the horizon, absorbed in some other, less wolf-related development. "Did you *hear* me?" I demanded. "There's a *wolf* out there!"

A stout mustachio with a cowboy hat and a lot of sun damage glared at me. "There aren't any wolves in Oklahoma, idiot." He turned back towards the forest and held a pair of binoculars up.

I strained my eyes to determine what on earth these idiots were all scoping out. Nothing. "Are you fucking *bird* watching?" I demanded. "Guys! One of your kids is literally about to be devoured by a wolf! C'mon," I said, taking a foot forward. "You fellas look like NRA members, who's got a concealed weapons permit? Let's go! Let's go!" I paused as I caught a glimpse of pink in the trees. I grabbed the mustachio's binoculars.

I spotted a girl. A *naked* girl. For unknown reasons, a svelte and nude twenty-something was playing peek-a-boo behind a tree a hundred yards away. "What the hell—" the guy grabbed his binoculars back and knocked me to the ground. He didn't punch me, just put his palm against my sternum and gave a solid push.

"Get yer own specs, dickhead."

I looked around frantically for help. Grampa employed several migrant workers in harvest season, and a few past that to prune and reset the vines before winter, but I didn't see any of them. They lived in a small shack at the other end of the vineyard, where they probably were at the moment.

Grampa usually asked them to lie low when visitors were around, as he had a longstanding policy of employing only illegal immigrants.

I dashed to the house and grabbed a woman's elbow. "Ma'am?" I said. "Please listen carefully. There's—" we all turned as more children started screaming at the top of their lungs. I loped behind the moms as they charged up the hill, strewing wine glasses behind them. Two pulled handguns out of their purses.

They reached the top of the hill, then screamed as a group, three sopranos and an alto. The wolf had grabbed a little girl by her pant cuffs and was playfully tugging her up a hill. The wolf didn't *seem* keen to eat the girl, although the hysterical child didn't seem to have arrived at that conclusion. She ferociously kicked her legs until the jeans came off, prompting the wolf to buck on its hind legs and fling the denim back and forth. The now pantsless little girl scrambled up the nearest windmill, while an entirely different group of kids figured out how to get on top of the barn roof, where they sat wailing and waving at their mothers like refugees in a flood. One child in the throes of a panic attack tried to climb up a kid on *top* of the barn, just in case.

A gun blast sounded off behind me. Grampa trudged up the slope gripping a revolver. He was *pissed*. "Git! You dirty mutt! *Git!*" He fired another round, missing the wolf entirely and blowing a chunk out of one of the windmill blades. The androgynous kid hugged the windmill and sobbed.

Grampa's face turned scarlet with rage. He cocked the gun and fired again, this time striking the barn. Children dropped from its roof, unsure of whether to be more afraid of the wolf, or the errant gunshots coming from the possibly-blind old man. A stream of urine dribbled down the side of the roof from one child still gripping the peak. "Grampa!" I yelled. "For God's sake *quit shooting!* You're going to blast one of the kids!"

"You lousy mongrel!" he screamed. He cocked the gun again but I ran over and tried to wrench it from him. "Gimme the gun!"

"No!" I yelled, doing my best to keep it pointed towards the ground.

"Gimme," he kept struggling, "the gun!"

I snatched the revolver from him and prepared to fire it at the wolf. But Grampa charged ahead, yanking a buckknife from a sheath on his belt. The old man looked like he was fully prepared to jump on the animal and start slashing.

"Grampa! Get out of the way so I can take a shot!"

"You miserable sack of dog shit!" he fumed. He kicked the wolf, catching it in the right haunch. The wolf swung around and growled, then spotted me. The beast entirely lost interest in the man who had just kicked it. Instead it surged towards me, growling and drooling as my shaking hands tried to get a bead on it.

I didn't have to. Behind me a chorus of rifles sounded off as the men in plaid stormed up the hill, weapons in hand. The wolf retreated into the forest as spurts of dirt cratered around it from more rifle shots. When it reached the edge of the trees it paused, turning back only for a moment to lock eyes with me.

It winked.

Chapter 5

"Don't try to make me think that I killed a man when I know that I killed a wolf!"

—Larry Talbot, *The Wolf Man*

You would think, between a wolf *and* naked woman interrupting the grape stomp, that Grampa and I would have much to discuss over breakfast the following morning. But that discounts how insanely calm my family can be in the face of weirdness. It might be regional. When the Pushmataha County Sheriff showed up after the fracas, he had explained that no wolves live in Oklahoma and so, logically, none of us had seen any. Everyone acceded to this rationality with varying levels of speed. All assembled witnesses arrived at a consensus of "strange coyotes," and a pledge to "keep on the lookout."

"I think," I said, scraping my breakfast around, "That I'm going to hold off on camping for a few days. What with the wolves," I added, by way of explanation.

"Reasonable," Grampa said. He continued thumbing through the newspapers.

I was still pretty confused about the relative danger of wolves at this point. I distinctly recalled from high school that wolves largely keep to themselves and purposefully avoid human interaction. Our textbook had been emphatic about

36

the wholly benign nature of wolves. But that was *also* in the era of Captain Planet, when environmentalism smoothly transitioned from a political goal to a minor religion. And while I concede even now that wolves serve a vital niche in the ecosystem, I had *also* seen one of them try to eat a fat kid. So I didn't know what to believe.

"Can I borrow your shotgun?" I asked. I did so with the same nonchalance I might employ when asking someone to pass the salt. Grampa nodded.

"Much obliged," I said, rising from the table. I walked to the front door and saw two rifles and a shotgun resting in the umbrella stand, along with a couple of canes and an umbrella. The configuration seemed to indicate that you might grab a rifle the same way you'd borrow an umbrella if the sky looked overcast. And these were just the easily accessible firearms—in his later life Grampa developed a habit of hiding guns around the house, "in case of emergencies." You might open an air vent and find a loaded revolver, or discover drapes hanging from an elephant gun. I slung a shotgun under my arm and walked through the vineyard into the woods.

The provisions from my botched attempt at camping two nights earlier had all been scattered and torn apart, but my car, thankfully, stood unmolested. I decided to visit the nearby unlabeled town I had cruised through twice already, once when backing over a wolf (as I now thought of them) and once on the return, when I'd seen the creepy locals having an evening funeral.

Which, at that exact moment, I assumed was some Protestant eccentricity. The backwoods of the

South and its allied satellites are chock full of novel takes on Christianity. First Church of the Screaming Jesus, Christ the Snakehandler, or Midnight Adventists—I didn't know the exact brand of grassroots Christianity, but supposed a nighttime funeral probably emerged from the custom of some peripheral fundamentalist sect.

Instead of hopping onto the highway I followed the serpentine routes of backwoods county roads which climbed through the Kiamichis before belching out onto a rolling field on the other side of the hills. Seeing Lycan on the horizon quite surprised me, as I had intended to visit, but not in a conscious, planned way. Even when trying my best I am garbage at directions, so having stumbled onto a vague inclination without any effort whatsoever seemed like a minor miracle. ("Minor miracle" being, in retrospect, a creepy synonym for "more than a coincidence." And it was.)

At the time, on the edge of the woods and a peripheral farm, the view was breathtaking. From the highway, the place had looked like a rusty practical joke, but from the foothills I thought I'd stumbled onto Shangri-La. I parked my car on the side of the road and began hiking toward the distant building, through a deep green field wrapping around the forest in the shape of a flat kidney. Similar grazing pastures terraced the side of the hills like golf courses easing down the contours of a mighty topographic map. Bales of hay dotted the landscape, capped with protective white plastic which affected the appearance of a giant marshmallow plantation.

I navigated down the grazing pasture, weaving

in and out of dumbfounded dairy cows. Even the livestock, some of the dumbest beasts on the planet, were tinged with magic. Every lactating mammal had a bell hung from its collar, which tinkled as I walked by. Aesthetic details like that are standard practice in Switzerland and parts of France and Germany, but such unnecessary expenditures are unheard of in the middle of the country. Outfitting cows with musical instruments made as much sense as painting their hooves blue to make them pretty. Perhaps it makes sense in a mountain environments, where a bell can help you locate a stray cow. But in the deep red states, where even now ancestral memories of sod houses still affect taste, and reign in pretensions, such frippery is unheard of. As I made my way down the alfalfa verandas, the arrhythmic clanging from cows drifted behind me like a bell choir of drunken angels.

From both the highway and its outer border on the field, Lycan looked like any other forgettable American hamlet. But as I approached on foot, I felt like a time traveler. For one thing, it didn't appear to have any chain restaurants, which seems like a small detail but actually isn't. The fact that I couldn't see a McDonald's or Starbucks or a Thank Goodness It's Fridays gave the approaching town an odd heaviness to it, like it had somehow mirrored the rest of America without joining in with it.

I watched a barber pole swivel at the intersection of Main Street and Bray Road. Passed an aging diner, a school yard, a doctor's office and a tiny grocery store. I had set foot in some outpost from the 1950's, colonizing the present day. It somehow had all the amenities of the twenty-first century, but without any of the blandness. I had not yet learned that secrecy can freeze a community in time, can make it draw into itself.

I ought to explain why my eyes were watering by the time I came upon the malt shop. I have numerous, idealized fuzzy memories of Hoople, the town of my birth. Fate ripped me from that comfortable existence at the age of twelve. From then until college my family moved from one large city to another, following Dad's promotions like a trail of nickels.

When we left Hoople some chunk of my being remained behind; a feeling of belonging quietly absent from all subsequent abodes. When Dad moved to Hoople he felt so eager to create a new life for himself, to meet people beyond the orbit of Nambersaw and his notorious father, that he endeavored and succeeded in befriending nearly every denizen of the town. My mother grew up there. I did not know what a "stranger" was until puberty.

I grew up in this environment, this cozy niche in the cosmos. If I got thirsty or skinned my knee, I would ring the doorbell of the closest house, and whoever opened it would give me a glass of water and a band-aid and probably cookies.

We left before I entered my teens. I recognize now that this early departure spared me from ever knowing the dark side of my home town. Nothing horrible, I imagine, just the little scrapes and bits of sadness that cling to anywhere people happen to live. The idyllic childhood friends I grew up with almost certainly took to underage drinking and underage pregnancy, so I suppose in a way it's nice that I left while, from my perspective, the town still had its innocence.

My family wrenched me from the blissful puddle of Hoople and jammed me into Dallas. Then Houston, Flagstaff, Sacramento, Seattle, and San Diego. The soft glow of neighbors and mom-and-pop general stores and a single, two-screen movie theater diminished. Ever since then my life has been one long attempt to feel like I belong some place, and I do not.

For that reason, whenever I enter a small town I feel a stab of loneliness. I pass through their Main Streets and see my own ghost, tracing the sidewalks of another life. I spot a group of kids at a crosswalk and recognize one specific guy as the one I would be friends with, who, in some parallel dimension, I *am* friends with. In the back of my mind, I look at all of these towns, and think, "Perhaps this one." I look, and tell no one, that deep down I plan to sink my feet deep into the red soil of my homeland and live in a small house with a wife and a dog I pretend to hate, and know my neighbors and radiate love like a sun god.

Of course, the anemoia wasn't intense enough to keep me from heading into the local malt shop and start interrogating the locals about Bigfoot. I had an undiscovered ape to research, after all.

I took a seat on one of the swiveling red stools and ordered a coffee. On my right sat a smiley old relic from the Nixon administration, reading a paper through half-moon spectacles and sipping a cup of coffee. He had on a green tweed blazer and a thin tie, neatly tucked beneath an argyle sweater vest. His face contained an abundance of wrinkles and a surplus of soft, geriatric skin. His lips were locked in a perpetual smile and his eyes remained arched, as if the tension alone kept the ample folds of his face from collapsing into a basset hound.

"Good morning," I said, leaning towards him.

"Mornin'," he said, still keeping his face taught by a perpetually upbeat expression.

"Recommend anything on the menu?"

He set his coffee down and reflected on this. "I like the grilled cheese sandwich, m'self."

"Thanks," I said, having established a warm rapport with my harmless menu query. "Ever seen Bigfoot?"

He looked at me like I'd just asked him what his favorite flavor of dynamite is. "What?"

"I'm collecting data about Bigfoot sightings in the area. Got any stories?"

I noticed several people looking up from their lunches. All eyes were on us. "None such, son. This is a quiet town, and a boring one." His lips pulled back further, more than should be possible, stretching his face into a weird, ancient parody of Dick Van Dyke. "What's a young feller like you doing hanging out here, eh? Well," he said, drawing the word out in a thick Dixie drawl, "if I were *yer* age, I'd be out chasin' skirts in a city some place. How 'bout I buy you lunch before you head out?" He winked at me.

"Oh, thanks," I said. "But I think I'll stick around for a little while. As I said, I'm doing a grant, and I need to ask folks about Bigfoot. Besides," I gestured to the diner, "I like it here. It might be a quiet town, but it sure is a pretty one." And so it was. The diner was an Art Deco malt shop, somehow perpetuated long past its origin in the fifties. It had a spotless black-and-white checkered floor, pink booths lining the walls, and swiveling stools at the counter topped with red vinyl. A juke box hummed away in the corner (playing oldies) and the walls contained enough polished aluminum to assemble a Japanese car.

I thought I was just being friendly by complimenting the man's town. I didn't realize that he was in the awkward position of trying to be kind *and* trying to dislodge me from Lycan like a champagne cork.

"Bigfoot, you say?" His smiled dropped and, as predicted, his face slackened into a vortex of pruney folds. After a moment of thought his eyebrows and smile sprung back into action, pulling his visage into order. "Nah, don't suppose anybody's ever seen a Bigfoot 'round here. You oughta head out to the Quachitas. Folks in yonder mountains are teeming with Bigfoot stories."

"Bigfoots are *everywhere* in the Quachitas," a waitress said, refilling the man's coffee. She smiled absently and adjusted her paper hat.

A middle-aged couple in one of the neighboring pink booths looked up. "Jack? Are you talking about Bigfoot?"

"No," he said, waving his arms. "Don't know a blessed thing about Bigfoot."

The man gestured to his wife and smiled. "That's funny, we were just talking about how we'd never seen Bigfoot, in fact know nothing *about* Bigfoot. Then, what did you say dear?"

His wife cleared her throat. "I said, I have a friend in," (her volume increased) "TISHOMINGO,

43

and she says everybody in TISHOMINGO has a story about Bigfoot."

"Fact is," said a man in neighboring booth, "Tishomingo actually *means* Bigfoot. In Cherokee."

I nodded slowly, appreciating the communal element of conversation in this particular whistle-stop, but also weirded out by the locals. I'm not a detective, but the ensemble of enthusiastic Bigfoot know-nothings struck me as odd. *The locals doth protest too much.*

"Well, okay," I said (to the entire restaurant). I scribbled my contact information on the back of a napkin and slid it to the old man seated next to me. "If you think of something pertinent to Bigfoot, I'm just a town over in Nambersaw."

"Sure, sure," the old man said. "Absolutely!"

I gulped down my coffee and stood up. "Lemme just pay for this," I said, rummaging through my pocket.

"On me!" said the codger known as Jack. "Don't you worry about it. Best hit the 'ol dusty trail, I reckon."

"Right," I said. "Okay." I walked towards the door, then stepped back as it flung open violently with a clang. A crazed lumberjack of a man stood there, nostrils flaring. When I say "lumberjack" I don't mean that he had a thick beard and a flare for plaid—although he had both. I mean he had a tangle of hair which looked like he had tried to comb it with an egg beater, and wild, angry eyes. He clomped into the diner in heavy, muddy boots, and towered over me by at least for inches despite his hunched posture.

"You," he said, fixating his berserk expression entirely on me. He slammed the door shut behind him with enough force it's a wonder the glass didn't shatter. He took another step towards me and jammed a finger into my sternum. "You're the bastard who ran over Lowell."

I looked around for help, but, astonishingly, the diner patrons who had been all too happy to discuss their lack of Bigfoot sightings mere moments ago were now ignoring the lunatic and myself with admirable concentration. The old guy at the counter peered into his coffee, fascinated, and I saw someone literally reading the back of a sugar packet, as if genuinely intrigued by the ingredients.[1]

I took a step back from the lunatic. "Sir, I've never met anyone named Lowell in my life."

"*Liar!*" he bellowed. "Don't you *dare*."

I looked around again for help, but the locals ignored us with a level of concentration usually reserved for medical school. "Sir," I said, putting my hands up, "I've never been here before. I'm not from here. I think you have the wrong guy."

"Last week," he said. "A blue Volvo. Do you drive a blue Volvo?"

I nodded. "That's… I hit what I thought was a coyote last Thursday. I didn't realize it was anyone's pet. I'm so sorry."

He clenched his fists and took another step towards me. "Well you *did*, boy. You did and you just got yourself into a whole world of hurt."

"Listen, sir, that was an honest accident. I really am sorry, and I'm happy to buy you a new dog, but—"

---

[1] "Sugar."

"Shut up," the man growled. He turned to face the rest of the diner, which dropped their farce and stared at him. "You heard it. This man killed Lowell." He choked up a little. "I'm justified in my actions. He's under *my* law, not yours." He turned back to me. "Outside. Now."

"What?" I asked. "What on earth are you talking about? I'm not going to *fight* you!"

The man snarled and lifted me by the collar of my shirt, then flung the door open. He dragged me outside and then slung his arm out, knocking me onto the sidewalk. I felt the heel of his boot clamp down on my throat. I looked up, expecting him to say something, but only felt his heel press down—he was going to crush my throat. I clawed at his boot, feeling consciousness begin to slip away.

Then I heard a loud *clang* and felt his heel release. A young woman, about my age, stood between us gripping a dented metal napkin dispenser. The man clutched the side of his face, swearing.

"Bitch!" he spat. "You *knew* Lowell!"

"Get out of here, Arno!" She held up the cudgel for another strike. "Git!"

The man scowled at her and then loped away, cupping his right cheek. He stopped at the corner of the diner and glared at us. "If you weren't kin I'd kill you where you stand! Might still," he said. His head swiveled to me and an expression of sheer rage washed over him, turning the shiner on his cheek scarlet. "*Your* days are numbered!" Then he ran past the edge of the diner and out of sight.

The girl stood there for several moments, evidently deciding whether or not the attacker would return. After deciding he wouldn't, she tossed the napkin dispenser onto some grass and held out her hand to help me up. "You okay?" she asked.

Most people, when they offer you a hand to assist you in standing, are doing so more as a matter of courtesy than any actual physical undertaking. Sort of like a handshake, except one of you is horizontal. I didn't think of this at the time, and grasping her hand, pulled her directly on top of me. She knocked the wind out of me, but it wasn't altogether unpleasant. We both stood up and brushed the dust off.

"I'm fine," I said, rubbing my throat. "Who *is* that guy? The town drunk?"

The girl put her hands in the pockets of her red sorority hoody. "That's Arno Phenris. The town bully. He lives in a shack out in the woods."

I prodded at the tenderness in my neck. "Sheesh! If that guy has the nerve to assault me in broad daylight, in a public restaurant, he's got to have some emotional issues or something. Thank God a girl was here to defend me. Who are you, by the way?"

"My name's Natalie," she said, studying me. "You're not from around here?"

"I'm not from around anywhere. But for now I'm staying with my grandfather, over in Nambersaw."

Natalie nodded. "Are you parked here?"

"No, I'm out east of town, past some farm."

She analyzed me with a curious expression. "Do you want a lift back to your car?"

Now it was my turn to study her. In all the excitement of the town nutjob trying to kill me I had not bothered to check whether or not she was hot. She was. Natalie had large hazel eyes so light in pigmentation they appeared to glow. Her lips curled up slightly at the ends, so that her resting state appeared to be one of playful smirking. And she had a great figure.

"Sure," I said. I followed her to a dark green pickup truck and clambered into the passenger seat. "I'm Saul, by the way. Thanks for saving me from the lunatic."

"Don't mention it." She pulled out of the parking lot and onto the road. "I'm back from college, and to be honest with you, there aren't a lot of people our age to hang out with around here. So saving your life was mostly selfish on my part."

"Well, now there's a lot of pressure for me to be interesting," I said. "I'm not sure I can live up to that."

"You'd be astonished how low my standards are right now," Natalie said. "This is a nice town. Nice people. But it's. . ." she searched for a word.

"Quaint?"

She laughed. "Yeah, you could call it that. I just did a study abroad program in Gévaudan, France. Yesterday I ran into this guy I knew from high school, and he asked me, 'Where's that?' When I told him it's near Avignon, he said, 'No, France. Where's that?'" She turned to look at me. "You know where France is, right?"

I shrugged. "Pretty sure it's still in Europe." She laughed again. She looked a little younger than me, maybe twenty-one or twenty-two, but she already had laugh lines at the edges of her eyes. It only amplified her allure. I found myself wondering how much you need to smile before laugh lines form. It seemed like a good sign.

"What college are you at?" I asked.

"Vanderbilt."

I gave a long, low whistle. "That's one of those really nice preppy schools out east, right?"

"It's in Tennessee."

"It sounds like the kind of place where people own boat shoes. I don't even know what boat shoes are, exactly."

Natalie laughed again. "You strike me as a cowboy boot-type guy." I wore sneakers, but cowboy boots sounded a lot cooler. I nodded. "How about you?" she asked. "Did you go to college?"

"Barely. I just graduated from Wiley College."

"Good school," she said, turning onto the town's Main Street.

I snorted. "I guess. I mean, my alma mater once awarded an honorary doctorate to Custer's horse. So I'm not sure if it's in the same category as Vanderbilt."

We chatted amicably for the drive as I navigated her to my car. She drove up behind it and turned to smile at me as she parked. "Saul, I'm here all summer and I don't have many friends I can have good chats with. I just don't really fit in here anymore. Do you want to hang out sometime?"

"Sure!" I said. I handed her my cell phone. "Put in your phone number and I'll text you."

"My mom is making lasagna tonight at our house," she said, handing her phone back to me. "Do you want to come over?"

I could scarcely believe my good fortune. I'm not bad looking, but Natalie was in an entirely different league. A woman with a weapons-grade bust and a smile that could knock a motorcyclist off his bike. That's not even including the fact that she owned a passport and went to a fancy school. Normally a guy like me acquiring a phone number from a girl like this took months of careful scheming and a lot of audio books designed to inflate self confidence.

I strained to look indifferent, as if I had a difficult time keeping all my many engagments straight in my mind. "Yeah," I said slowly, "I could do tonight. What time?"

"Around seven o'clock, it's pretty casual." She leaned over me to open her glove compartment and fish out a paper and a pen. All at once I had a staggering sexual epiphany. In college I mostly dated blonde girls ranging in body type from "skinny" to "ludicrously thin." I had not yet figured out that someone could be pretty without being sexy, and it turns out what I personally find sexy is *curves*. Natalie had those in spades. She was by no means overweight, but definitely more voluptuous than the coltish young ladies who had bunked with me at Wiley. As she fumbled around her glove compartment the v-neck of her shirt hinted at an epic topography of cleavage underneath. She returned to her seat without even touching me, but the near-contact made erotic goose bumps break out on my arms. Plus a fairly impressive erection.

"Here," she said, handing me a note. "422 Bray Road."

"Okay," I said. "But just because I'm meeting your parents doesn't mean I'm ready for commitment, okay?"

"That's good, because I have a boyfriend." Of course she did. Girls like her *always* had boyfriends.

"Hey, good for *you*," I said, climbing out of her pickup. "See you tonight!"

*

So all this stuff happened well before the invention of Tinder, where you can judge huge swaths of people, for hours on end, without ever leaving the comfort of your bathroom. Just sitting there on the toilet like a Victorian aristocrat, swiping through pictures of human beings. Who, if you met in person two beers deep at a bar, you would almost certainly try to have sex with. But again, by the time I first visited Lycan, most of us still used our phones for calling people, or possibly to play an extremely pixilated game called "Snakes." Smartphones and hookup apps had not yet been invented.

By the time I graduated college people still viewed "online dating" as very new and novel and the last resort for ugly people frightened of sunlight. Nobody met on the Internet, or at least admitted to it. Throughout college myself and my peers (read: drunk horny guys) found dates in older, more traditional ways. Specifically, by getting so hammered in a bar that we could summon the nerve to approach, and possibly even speak to, a woman. Girls, at this point in human history, would actually *go to bars to meet men*. They would just stand around in clumps, like gazelle, waiting for us to get drunk enough to talk to them.

If you didn't like drinking (for some reason) any college campus teemed with enough horny young

51

people you could more or less walk in any direction and eventually collide with. Then you could go get coffee and, hopefully, get naked together in a dorm room. Several of my friends who are now not only respectable attorneys but so prosperous that they've upgraded to Episcopalian met their significant others by blundering into them, stoned or drunk, while struggling to kick a hackey sack.

So driving to Natalie's house to meet her, and her family, felt atavistic. It seemed like a flashback to my high school years, when mobile phones were large gray bricks exclusively used by Wall Street traders and drug dealers, with approximately as much battery power as a can of ravioli but vastly more expensive.

In my high school days we didn't even have alcohol as a crutch to approach women—we had to man up and ask budding young ladies for their phone number, dead sober, and hope the girl wouldn't laugh at us. If she did, the law required us to run away from high school and become a monk or circus freak.

If we snagged their digits, we'd later call their house, and their dad would pick up. In every instance of this ritual the father would be a Vietnam vet with a shovel and six acres behind his house, and he might even slip that tidbit into his conversation with you before finally handing the phone over to his daughter. Then you would awkwardly ask her to go to a movie and, hopefully, wind up groping each other afterwards in a parking lot with all the magical romance of two drowning people trying to climb each other to stay afloat. That's how I got my first kiss. I probably would have lost my virginity to the same girl soon after had her older brother, whose physique resembled an angry refrigerator, not escorted me to my car one evening and ominously said, "Have a good time at the movies. Just remember: whatever you do to *her* I do to *you*."

I thought about this as I pulled up to 422 Bray Road and scoped out the house. It was a big Victorian-style two story with upper middle class evidence pelted all over it: green shutters, a well-maintained roof, an iron street lamp standing sentry at the driveway, and a stately elm with an old swing dangling underneath. Not having met Natalie's parents, I could already tell by the meticulously tended property that they would rather jog naked around their neighborhood than let their lawn get scraggly.

The whole place made me feel underdressed, and I wished I had worn my button-up shirt instead of my ironic t-shirt. (A blue shirt with a large Union Jack flag plastered across the front, with "Greece" stenciled in bold underneath.) I checked myself in the mirror and struggled to preen a little. I inherited my jet black hair from my Choctaw grandmother, and its eternal cowlick from my father. The cowlick waved indignantly from my scalp, taunting my efforts to comb it. I also get my brown eyes from my grandmother, the color of wet leather. They're dark enough that in certain lighting I appear to have two gigantic pupils. I'm told they're horrifying to behold if you've ingested a gram or three of hallucinogenic mushrooms.

I walked up to the door and read the tidy, understated brass placard above the doorbell: "Rougarou." I buzzed and a man in a white lab coat swung the door open. "You must be Saul," he said, ushering me in. "I'm Natalie's father, Maurice. She's cleaning up from the ranch. Come on in." I took my shoes off and followed him into the family room, which I assumed these people called a "parlor" and sat across from him on a creaky leather sofa. Logs in the fireplace crackled nearby, the maiden fire of the year's cooler season.

"Would you like any cider?" he asked. I nodded. "Cally?" he called, turning his head towards the kitchen. An aproned lady with highlighted hair leaned out of the doorway. "Honey, why don't you come out and meet Natalie's friend? And would you bring some cider with you?"

"Oh! Yes!" she piped.

Maurice smiled calmly and stared at me, sizing me up. Trying to determine whether or not I was screwing his daughter. I anticipated this, and felt surprisingly unrattled. In fact I rather liked the guy. He had brushed brown hair, graying at the temples, and a thin, well-trimmed mustache. Pulling off a mustache is tough business. Unless you're a cop or a fireman you run a high risk of looking like a pervert. But his cheeks folded in dull jowl lines which seemed to justify the lip rug. Crinkles sprouted from the corners of his eyes, although I would not quite call them laugh lines. "Sympathy lines," I suppose. The minute folds of someone who's helped deliver a child and pulled up the sheet over a heart attack victim on the same day. He peered at me over a pair of rectangular reading glasses.

"So you're either a pediatrician or a butcher," I said.

He smiled and tilted his head. "No, why would

you think that?"

I shrugged. "This will sound corny, but you look like the embodiment of benevolent childhood authority figures. I just assumed."

He laughed, dislodging the spectacles to rub his eyes. "Nothing that specific, although it's nice of you to say. I'm the town doctor." Mrs. Rougarou stepped into the room with a tray of steaming mugs. "Oh, sit," she scolded, pressing down on her husband's shoulder before he could rise. She placed the tray on the coffee table and leaned forward to shake my hand. "Hello, I'm Accalia, but call me Cally."

"Solomon Heinrich," I said, shaking her hand. "Pleased to meet you."

She sat down next to her husband on the couch, not touching, but angling her knees his direction. He laid an arm along the back of the sofa, lightly resting his fingers on her shoulder. "Be careful, dear, the cider is hot."

"Thank you," I said, picking my mug up and blowing across its steamy surface.

"What do you do, Mrs. Rougarou?"

"I teach third grade," she offered. She laughed, like "third grade" was a cute punch line. I force myself to chuckle. "And yourself?"

"I'm an anthropologist."

Both Rougarous nodded enthusiastically. "Doing what?" Dr. Rougarou asked.

"Well," I said, laughing nervously, "I graduated a couple of months ago, and for the next few months I'm out here in southeastern Oklahoma looking for Bigfoot."

"For Bigfoot?" Mrs. Rougarou asked. "How. . ." she turned to her husband in search of vocabulary aid. "How very *interesting*."

"Find anything of note?" he asked.

"Yes," I said. "But not for several days."

Natalie descended the stairs, hair recently blow-dried and flopping against her red hoody. When I met her earlier that day she had not been wearing makeup, but seemed to have prepped herself for dinner, and, I hoped, for me. "Hi, Natalie."

"Hi Saul." She glanced between myself and her parents, searching for traces of tension or awkwardness. Finding none, she sat down on the same couch as me, but at the opposite end.

I took a sip of cider and reflexively smiled. The tang from some kind of spice, or maybe cranberry juice, pleasantly caught the pockets of my mouth. "This is delicious, Mrs. Rougarou."

"It's an old family recipe. Does your family live around here, Solomon?"

"Please call me Saul," I said. "Not my immediate family, but my dad's from around here. His brother and father live in Nambersaw."

"Saul's grandfather owns Nashoba Vineyards," Natalie offered.

"Really?" Dr. Rougarou asked, sitting up. "That's amazing!" He walked over to a bar at the end of the room and pulled out a bottle of Friends in Merlot Places, the signature wine of Nashoba Vineyards. "We keep your whole stock, see?" To prove it, he displayed the various bottles. Our malbec, Grapes of Wrath. Grand Finwicke, a pinot noir. And, my favorite, Tipsy Golem Chardonnay. He even had a bottle of La Vino Loco Cabernet Sauvignon, discontinued two years prior. "Good stuff, good stuff," he muttered, returning to his seat.

The doorbell rang. Natalie hopped up. "I'll get it."

"Where did you and Natalie meet?" Mrs. Rougarou asked. "Last—"

"Dad?" Natalie said, returning moments later, pale and serious. She gestured to two teenagers behind her. Boys, probably sixteen or so. The one nearest me had a bloody hand wrapped in a t-shirt, while the other wore a pair of torn jeans with a large gash running down his calf.

Dr. Rougarou jumped up. "What happened?" He dashed to the two youths and inspected their wounds.

The boy with a bleeding hand swallowed. "We were. . ." his voice warbled, trying to hold back tears. "We were out near Arno Phenris's place—"

"Still in the town limits!" his companion blurted out.

"—and we got attacked."

The other kid nodded. "I think we might need stitches. We were still in the town," he added.

"Did they bite you?" The boys shook their heads.

"Just scratched us, sir."

Dr. Rougarou nodded and stood up. "You'll need stitches all right. Natalie? Would you go get the black handbag out of my office?"

"What's going on?" Mrs. Rougarou asked. "Maurice?"

"Why don't you boys go sit down in the kitchen?" He smiled amicably. "It'll be harder to sew you up if you're standing. There's still some cider on the stove, I think, so help yourselves. Hey, everything's fine, okay?" he patted their shoulders, then tilted them towards the kitchen. They nodded and walked out of the room. Dr. Rougarou faced his wife. "I don't know. It seems that," he glanced at me for a moment, "that Arno's dogs have expanded their territory."

"They *attacked* the kids?"

He shrugged. "Arno has smart dogs. If they meant to kill the kids, they wouldn't be here right now."

"This is an outrage!" She stood up and balled her fists. "Completely unacceptable! If Arno is going to have his, his *dogs* running around all the time, he needs to keep them on his property!"

He threw his hands up. "I know, I know." Natalie returned with his black satchel. "Thank you, sweetie. Why don't you show Solomon your room? I'd like to talk to your mother."

"Okay," she said, grabbing my hand and walking towards the stairs.

"Open door policy!" he yelled.

I followed her up to her room, not sure of what to say or do with myself. "Is everything okay?"

"Oh, yeah," she sighed, shutting the door behind us. "Arno Phenris is just a crummy guy, that's all. Those kids are lucky they didn't get seriously hurt."

She kept her room generally neat, with an occasional towel or pair of jeans draped over something. Framed, black and white pictures of European cities hung on the walls. The air hung thick with humidity from the shower she took earlier in the adjoining bathroom, which made everything smell wonderful. Of exotic shower gels and scrub brushes I know nothing about, of girl.

"Phenris is the guy whose dog I ran over, right?"

She nodded. "Hey!" she said, changing subjects, "Would you like to borrow any books? For when you're out in the woods?"

"Sure!" She stepped over to a pile of texts beside her bed and selected a stack of four. *The Great Gatsby*, *The Prince of Tides*, *Brave New World* and *Der Rosafarbene Ritter*. "Thanks," I said, glancing at the titles. "Is this last one in English?"

She nodded. "It's an English translation of a tenth century Saxon epic about a knight, told from the perspective of his magic sledge hammer. I had to read it in France for—"

We heard her parents yelling outside. She ran to the window and I quietly followed, glancing over her shoulder to the couple arguing on the driveway below. Her mother stood hands-on-hips across from an exasperated Dr. Rougarou.

"He's your *cousin*, Maurice!"

"I know that!" he snapped. He took a deep breath and collected himself. "Listen, honey, they're very cunning. I'm going to put the traps in plain sight, just to let them know we mean business. I'm not out to hurt anyone."

Mrs. Rougarou threw her hands up in the air. "Then don't go storming off to set bear traps!"

"Accalia! Arno and his lot have violated some very old, very important boundaries. He needs to know they're still enforced. Nothing more, just a warning." He leaned over and picked up a couple of gleaming metal contraptions, dropping them in his truck bed.

"Oh, like the Wargson boys got a warning tonight?"

"Hey," I said slowly, "What exactly—"

Natalie grabbed my face and kissed me. With tongue. A lot. After a few moments I staggered back, grinning and disoriented. "He*llo*," I said, putting a hand on her waist.

She opened the door to the bedroom and stepped into the hall, hips swaying. "I'm so glad you came over tonight, Saul." She walked towards the stairs with me in tow. "And I hope you enjoy the books."

"I'm sure I will," I mumbled, dazed. I blindly followed her down the stairs and to the front door as she tugged me through the house by the tips of my fingers.

"Have fun looking for Bigfoot!" She threw her hands around my neck and kissed my cheek. "You'll call me soon?"

I nodded, dumbfounded.

"Good! See you later!" She opened the front door and pushed me out.

Her parents turned to face me. Their lips pried apart in forced, artificial smiles.

"Off already?" Mrs. Rougarou asked.

"It seems so."

Dr. Rougarou grinned and nodded like a neck injury victim. "Good to meet you, Solomon! You come over anytime. Have some more cider!"

"That sounds nice," I stammered.

"Bye!" Natalie called from the porch.

I climbed into my car and started the ignition. Her parents put their arms around each other and yelled "Bye now!"

I drove off. The Rougarou family continued waving until they were no longer in sight.

Chapter 6

"And the wolf walked round and round the tree, looking at them with hungry eyes."

—Sergei Prokofiev, *Peter and the Wolf*

From the outside, Grampa's winery appeared to be a standard red barn, but the inside looked like a science fiction scene from the Gilded Age. Four huge copper drums dominated its interior, with shining wheels, valves and pressure gages sprouting in between. Chalkboards lined the walls from floor to ceiling. Mazes of chemistry equations, soil Ph levels, and barely legible formulas spilled across the inky background in the frantic white handwriting of a mad scientist.

I stood at the top of a wobbly latter, emptying a bag of oak chips into the vat used to concoct Grand Fenwicke pinot noir. After unloading them into the primordial drink below I shut the hatch and screwed its submarine-style wheel down. At Grampa's behest, I earned my room and board by working at his vineyard. I agreed to it purely because I reasoned I would eventually elect to take my chances with the wolves over being cooped up with the old man. If I survived the woods, I might just find Bigfoot.

Beneath me, Grampa Rabbi scuttled in between the vast drums, checking pressures and temperatures. "Are you sticking around for night-breakfast?" he asked. "Your Uncle Amos is coming over."

"Night-breakfast?" I asked.

"I only eat breakfast." He lit up a cigar and took several puffs. For a moment, his billowy white beard faded into the cancerous fug of smoke.

"What?"

"I eat three meals a day, all breakfast."

"Oh, I said." It explained the monotony of his refrigerator and freezer. They looked like a munitions storage of sausage, bacon and eggs. Which desperately needed defrosting. Ice stalactites hung down from the top, encasing old waffles like frozen cavemen. "That's stupid," I said.

"Breakfast is the most important meal," he pressed. I couldn't tell if he was joking or actually thought there might be some health benefit from eating the first meal of the day three times daily. "Besides, I *like* breakfast. It's my favorite." The cigar cloud enveloping him thickened. He smoked enough in his barn the wine probably had trace elements of nicotine; it may well have been his secret ingredient.

"I'll be there," I said, descending the latter.

"Good. Be sure to wear your kipah."

"What? No."

"If you live in my house you abide by my rules. We show our respect to Elohim by wearing a kipah. To signify that He's always above us." Grampa put his hand over his black cowboy hat, and looked up towards God, to illustrate his point. He smiled and reached into his pocket to withdraw a circular scrap of cloth, then tossed it to me.

I stared down at the skull cap. "Are you kidding? This is just a mangled baseball cap. What did you do, lobotomize the bill with blunt scissors? It still has the Dallas Cowboys insignia."

He threw his hands up in exasperation. "What if I did? I always wear my rabbinical Stetson. *I* don't need a kipah for day-to-day use."

"Well, neither do I. I'm not Jewish."

"*Oh yes you are*," Grampa said, raising his eyebrows and thrusting the cigar stub between words like a shank. "And Jews cover their heads. You don't like the kipah I made?" he shrugged. "Find a cowboy hat. Or a fez. Frankly I don't care, Solomon. But that's the house rule, and so long as you partake of my generosity, you abide my regulations." I grumbled and slapped the mutilated baseball cap onto the site of my future bald spot. Grampa nodded and pointed his cigar at another bag of oak chips. "Can you take care of that?" he asked.

I sighed. "Sure thing." For years, Grampa had avoided purchasing expensive oak barrels by instead running firewood through a wood chipper and dumping the contents into the vats. He would remove the woody flakes after a few weeks, leaving behind a tasty "oak barrel finish."

I moved the ladder to the Grapes of Wrath drum and climbed up with a bag over my shoulders. I cranked open the hatch and began dumping wood chips into the mass of grapes beneath. Grampa looked up. "Solomon!" he shouted. "Are you putting in oak chips?!"

"Yes?" I asked.

"Stop! Stop!" he screamed, turning red. I pulled the bag back and watched chunks of tree drizzle to the floor. "*Dammit!*" he yelled, slamming his hat down. "Dammit, Solomon! You moron!"

"What?" I exclaimed.

63

"*Oak* chips go in the pinot noir. *Mulch* goes in the malbec. Dammit!" he picked the Stetson up again and threw it against the wall. "Skim them out!" He stormed to the back of the barn and returned with a pool maintenance net. "Fish 'em out," he growled, thrusting it towards me. "Clean it up!"

I caught the net and glared at him. "How the hell was I supposed to know that, Grampa?" I skimmed an island of chips off the top and dumped them to the floor. "You should have been more specific."

"What?!" he exclaimed. He spun his arms around wildly, gesturing to the blackboards around us. "I guess I labor under the delusion that my descendants have the same common sense *I* have." He stamped over to a wall and pounded his fist against an equation, knocking chalk dust onto his faux Lubovitch attire. "Here! See this? Can you *read?*" Above his fist, a small chart located within the sprawl of chalkings indeed clarified which wood adulterated which wine.

"Sorry," I said, flinging a clump of purple shavings near his feet, "I guess I'm not as used to getting pertinent information from bathroom graffiti as you are. I'll try and get into that habit."

Grampa gave the ladder a tiny kick, balling his fists. "Don't you talk back, smartass! I would've socked your dad for a dumb mistake like that. But I would've knocked his *lights* out for talking back."

"Yes," I said, dropping the net to the floor. "Dad has given me a full briefing on your marvelous parenting techniques."

"He turned out okay."

"You told your children that when ice cream

trucks play music it's because they're out of ice cream, and they're signaling other trucks for more."

Grampa ignored this walk down memory lane. "Did you get it all?" he asked. I nodded. He put his hands on his hips and stared at the drum. "If it alters the flavor, we'll call it Grapes of Wrath: Censored Version, or something like that. Then go back to the regular formula next year."

I walked to the mound of wood chip bags and scrutinized the correct type. "Grampa, this is literally gardening mulch."

He nodded. "Gives it a zingy smoothness. It's like storing it in four different sorts of barrels, all at once." He re-lit his stogie, humming. The seething anger which had possessed him moments earlier entirely disappeared, as if he no longer recalled the incident. Which I presumed likely considering the man's age. He disappeared, trailing smoke, and I finished dumping tree guts into the wine drums.

After a shower and a change of clothes, I popped into the kitchen to find my uncle seated at the adjoined dining room table, hunched over a wine glass. "Hello, Amos," I said, positioning myself across from him.

He looked up from his wine and smiled, an unfetching gesture which looked like fishhooks lifting his gum flaps from the surrounding pudge. "Howdy, nephew." He had not aged gracefully. According to his ex-wives Amos had been a muscular youth, but his post-tavern career as a rodeo clown eventually pried the meat from his bones, which now hung like flaps of rubber beneath his skin. His neck looked like a deflating intertube someone had looped around a spine. "Your Dad called me a few days ago to let me know you would be in this part of the country. He wants me to keep an eye on you." We laughed. "What brings you here?"

I shifted uncomfortably and forced myself to smile through the embarrassing job description. "I'm on a grant to look for Bigfoot."

Amos leaned back in the seat, creaking the wood. "Ha!" he said, eyes glittering. I imagine the eyes are what confused and ultimately snagged his exes. Neither lid ever opened entirely, giving him a listless, absent look. Yet they somehow magnificently twinkled with mischief. As if a man of magic and destiny were expertly hiding beneath the layers of loser and flab.

"A grant!" he rumbled. He reached over and slapped me on the shoulder. "There you *go*, Solomon! You sweet-talked a fistful of cash to look for the 'ol Green Hills Monster? Attaboy!" I smiled. If Amos took pride in imagining my exploits as a clever scam, so be it.

"How is life as a rodeo clown?"

He shrugged, unsettling layers of fleshy debris on the tectonic plates of his shoulders. "It's fun, I guess. I meet interesting people, get to travel, work outdoors. A little taxing at times, though. I really ought to figure out what I want to do when I grow up."

The door to the back porch flung open and Grampa teetered into the house. The sun set in the windows behind him. "Shalom, Amos!" he said, walking over to pat his son on the head. "How are you, my boy?"

Amos turned towards him and grinned. "If I

was any better I'd be you, Pops."

"Haha! Glad to hear it!" Grampa walked to the kitchen and opened the refrigerator. "I was thinking omelets, with some honey-nut Cheerios for dessert. Objections?"

"Sounds delicious," I offered.

"Good lad," he said, cracking an egg over a frying pan. "Would you set the table for us?"

"Sure."

Amos swished his wine glass around. "So what does Bigfoot hunting entail, exactly?"

"Fieldwork and interviews," I said, putting a place mat in front of him. "Eventually I'll camp out in the Kiamichis or Quachitas, looking for tracks and hair samples. The rest of the time I'll interview locals about encounters they might have had."

Amos grew suddenly serious. "Fieldwork?" He leaned forward. "A word of advice? Stick to interviews, Sauly. I saw something out there once. I have friends who have. Invite them here, buy them a drink. Buy them another and they'll tell you about it."

"What's wrong with the woods?" I asked.

"For one thing, if you stumble out of the woods into someone's farm, you're liable to get shot."

"Yeah," I agreed. I put plates and glasses on the table. "I nearly hit a tripwire on the way to Hugo. Marijuana farm."

"They're surprisingly dense in these parts. And you'll find we're not for want of meth labs." He raised his eyebrows. "Be aware of your surroundings."

"Solomon?" Grampa asked, agitating the frying pan's contents with a spatula, "Did you set four places?"

I looked at the table. "No," I said. "Three. Is someone else coming?"

He smiled at me. "I like to set a place for your grandmother."

Grandma Gladys had died ten years ago, so I wasn't entirely sure if he meant this as an endearing gesture, or as the vanguard of dementia. I opted to keep quiet about it.

Grampa added another egg to the frying pan and smiled, looking out through the window. "Your grandmother was so *lovely.* Do you remember Gladys, Solomon?"

"A little, Grampa," I lied. I collected another place setting from the kitchen.

He tossed some cheese onto the forming omelet. "What a beautiful, decent woman she was. My!" He shook his head and smiled. "I hope you snatch someone like her someday." He glanced my way. "Preferably Jewish."

Grampa Rabbi's love for his wife was a redeeming quality he developed later in life. He married my grandmother, Gladys Black Kettle, entirely to acquire Nashoba Vineyards as a dowry from her full-blood Choctaw father. For the first two decades of their marriage she was only the organic clause in a contractual obligation necessary to obtain the property.

Yet suddenly, more than two decades after their wedding day, Grampa fell in love with her. I doubt the woman was ever very fetching, but based on pictures by fifty she looked part mule. Despite this, a deep and abiding love smoldered and burned in his crusty heart. He dropped all womanizing and fell into a schoolboy crush, which snowballed each year into increasing degrees of adoration and devotion. All this at the age of fifty-two.

He had been a lousy husband until that time. But when the twenty-year interregnum separating vows from love finally ceased, the couple enjoyed a prolonged honeymoon which stretched for another twenty-five. By then my father and aunt had moved away from Nambersaw and rarely visited, but Amos saw the transformation first-hand. He watched the ogre he grew up with succumb to a moon-struck adulation of his mother, watched him repent of and make up for two decades of neglect.

My first memory of Grampa was at Gladys's funeral. Dad had not visited Nambersaw since before my birth, but returned for her his mother's internment. The old codger stood trembling in the graveyard, closed to hysterics, weeping and stroking the casket. At that moment, my father finally saw some good in the man, caught a glimmer of Skywalker in the Darth Vader who sired him. We resumed visiting the family patriarch that summer, returning regularly to Nambersaw for Hanukkah and Yom Kippur. (Which, fortunately, we could schedule whenever we wanted, since no one including Grampa knew their actual dates.)

I sat down at the table. Amos fished a green kipah out of his pocket and plopped it on the back of his head. *"Put on a hat,"* he mouthed, as Grampa approached the table with a plate of omelets and carton of orange juice.

I shrugged. *"I don't have one,"* I mouthed back, having already thrown away the hideous skullcap Grampa fashioned from a baseball hat. Amos nodded and pulled a bright blue kipah out of his other pocket and tossed it to me. I slung it on just as Grampa sat down.

"Omelets!" he announced. "With red peppers, cheese, and bacon." I shoveled one onto my plate and began sawing it apart. "Would you pray for us, Amos?" he asked, as I deposited a bite in my mouth.

"Sure, Pops," Amos said. He took a deep breath and bowed his head. "Adonai, we thank you for this food. May trespassers be struck down by lightning, and may the television lineup be fruitful. Amen." The Heinrich Family Prayer, verbatim.

"Amen," Grampa said, scooping an egg off the serving dish.

We looked up as someone knocked on the back door. "Come in!" Grampa yelled. Three of the Mexican workers from the edge of the vineyard stepped in. The one in the middle respectfully held his hat in his hands. The man to his left held a flashlight, and the one on his right clutched a pitchfork. "What is it, Pedro?" Grampa asked.

"Señor," Pedro said, stepping forward, "this night. . . This night we see el lobo in the vineyard."

"El lobo?"

Pedro turned to the man on his right, a stocky tan fellow in a t-shirt and jeans. He shrugged. "Eh. . . the wolf? We see the wolf."

Pedro nodded. "Si, Señor. *The wolf.*"

Grampa raised his eyebrows. "And?"

The three Mexicans rapidly conferred amongst themselves. Pedro flung his hands out and they fell quiet. "Señor, el lobo, he is near. We see the foots. . ." he gestured to his friend again.

"Feet marks," he said. "Near this."

Grampa stood up calmly. "Can you show me?" They nodded. We followed the workers out the back door to the side of the house. They pointed to a patch of mud near the air conditioning unit. Grampa squatted down to observe a couple of fresh paw prints.

He looked at them quizzically. "Just a coyote, boys. No need to be alarmed." The three Mexicans responded in loud Spanish, pointing at the paw print.

Pedro silenced them. He walked away from the mud patch to the house, gesturing to another set of tracks beneath the window overlooking the living room. "Here," he said. He pointed to the window sill itself, more than four feet off the ground. "And here."

Grampa walked over and quietly scrutinized the site. He ran a hand along the window sill and drew it up, looking at the fresh mud on his finger tips.

He turned to face Pedro and arched an eyebrow. "Looks like we have a pet." He glanced down at his muddy finger before rubbing it against his palm, then reaching into his jacket to withdraw a cigar. "And a damned curious one at that."

Chapter 7

*"A clear cold morning with high wind: we caught in
a trap a large gray wolf, and last night obtained in the
same way a fox who had for some time infested the
neighborhood of the fort."*

—Meriwether Lewis

I woke up the next morning in a wave of
nauseating, guilt-ridden aimlessness. I had
experienced several such moments in the months
following graduation, although their rapidly
increasing frequency was beginning to addle me. It's
difficult to spend sixteen years of your life on a
standardized academic track only to be dumped at
the end of it with a diploma and a vague sense that
you ought to be amounting to something. Most of my
friends obtained jobs, got married, went to grad
school or enjoyed some combination thereof. I
journeyed to Little Dixie to search for an elusive,
probably non-existent ape.

And I wasn't even *looking* for Bigfoot. Not at the
moment, anyway. I was lying in the upstairs guest
bedroom of my grandfather's Georgian ramshackle,
waking up near noon. I walked to the bathroom and
sat down in the shower, slowly collecting my
thoughts.

Did wolves even *live* in Oklahoma? I had been
mentally referring to the creatures in the woods as

wolves, but previously thought none lived in the region. Everyone except Grampa and the Mexicans seemed confident they were coyotes, albeit unusually dangerous ones.

I stepped out of the shower and dried off before tending to the embarrassing ritual of shaving. (At the time I could grow half a mustache and some black moss on the underside of my chin. If I didn't shave I looked a bit like a child molester, but the necessary act of shaving seemed superfluous given the small amount of actual hair growth.)

Clean and clean shaven, I walked to my room and dialed Cindy's home number. Her father answered. "Kampton residence."

"Mr. Kampton? This is Saul Heinrich. How are you?"

"I'll get Cindy."

"No, wait!" I heard Leonard inhale a belabored breath over the phone. "Actually, I wanted to talk to you."

"About what?"

"Well, I was thinking, as a taxidermist and hunter you probably have a decent idea of the wildlife in this area." I waited for him to agree with me, but he didn't. I pressed on. "So I thought you would be a good person to call. Are there still wolves in Oklahoma?"

"Wolves?"

"Yes, wolves. I remember hearing they used to be prevalent throughout North America, but are much smaller in numbers now. Are there still any in this part of the country?"

"Lemme think." Three minutes passed as he waited for a commercial break on the other line.

When a Pepsi ad sounded off he began talking. "Red wolves were indigenous to this region, but they were declared extinct in the wild in the eighties. The last red wolves spotted in the United States were in this area, in the Quachita Mountains I think, around 1930. If there are any left, they've interbred with coyotes to the point of non-existence."

"Wow," I said, "thank you, that was the exact information I wanted. I ask because I'm pretty sure I *saw* a wolf in the Kiamichis, actually several times."

"You undoubtedly saw a coyote," he said, in a tone which suggested his assessment of me had just slipped down another notch.

"I'm not sure about that. It looked bigger and healthier than a coyote."

"Saul, listen: if red wolves do not exist, how could you have seen a red wolf?"

I decided to skip the argument and its entangling fallacies. "Good point. Okay, thanks Mr. Kampton. Say hello to Cindy for me."

"Yeah." He hung up the phone.

A new idea occurred to me: finding a presumably extinct species, though not as glamorous as tranquilizing a Sasquatch, would still make a splash in the scientific community. I might win an award, at least get a lecture or two. I could theoretically expand my current search to include the species. If I got a few good photographs and a hair sample, that might be enough. In fact, it might even be *possible*, given that I thought I'd seen such a creature.

I decided I had been too lax in my bigfoot research. My next trip to the woods would be for three weeks. After a hearty noon breakfast I drove into Nambersaw to buy some camping supplies.

And sleeping pills.

*

These are my tips on Bigfoot hunting:

Wander into the woods. It goes without saying that you should find a secluded chunk of forest away from the sounds of passing automobiles that would otherwise drive skittish primates further inward. Continue wandering until you find a selection of trees which feels like the sort of place you personally would hang out at if you were a Sasquatch. If you suspect there are bloodthirsty wolves patrolling the area, I recommend you take a machete and a friend who runs slower than you. (I didn't bring a friend with me—unless you counted my machete.)

I used a compass and map at the time, but now you could probably use a GPS coordinator on your phone to mark your whereabouts. Erect a tent and set up camp. If you think there's a significant risk of wild animals devouring you in your sleep, build your campsite in the tree using a series of hammocks and sleeping bags. Now, two to three times a day, make a huge circle through the forest around your campsite, with a radius of about a mile. I'm not sure what that would make the circumference—anyone with a basic understanding of geometry (not me) could probably calculate it using *pi* or something. If you're already bringing a slower friend as wolf bait, why not ask if he's good at math?

I did my patrols twice a day. Once at dawn, and once in the afternoon. The surveillance was not to find an actual Bigfoot (surely one could hear me coming) but to check for tracks or other primate indicators.

Bring a good book. I don't care how smart you think you are, or how "deep" the junk on your coffee table is. The human brain can only speed through productive thought for so long before you hit a mental screen saver program and keep thinking about the same stupid subject in endless feedback loops. Whereas, if you have a ready supply of reading material, you can potentially pull a Walden. I had at my disposal the tomes Natalie lent me.

Normally I dislike books with notes in the margins, but while living in the forest I relished those ponderous scribbles. I followed which words she underlined, the question marks at the end of certain passages and the occasional exclamatory phrase following a chapter. It felt like a conversation.

Which was nice, as I could barely communicate with her otherwise. It had been two weeks and three days since I set out to live in a tree, and I only stopped by the vineyard once a week for supplies. I activated my mobile phone sparingly, for fear I would need it in an emergency but find it lacking juice. Once a day I would turn it on for half an hour, dispatch a text message her way, and hope she responded. The result was a flirtatious but painfully slow correspondence.[2] All the more so because, as she often pointed out, we were *just friends.*

At 3:00 my scuffed Casio watch chirped, prompting me to my afternoon Bigfoot track vigil. I set the dog-eared copy of *The Prince of Tides* down on

---

[2] Needless to say, this was all before camera phones and sexting.

my folding chair, grabbed a protein bar and a bottle of water, and started walking. Through a cluster of cedars, past the charred remnants of some elms, over some boulders, down to the creek.

I took particular time with the creek. Although I could not predict *where* Bigfoot might quench his thirst, it stood to reason he might hit the creek up. So every day I spent time combing up and down the muddy banks, looking for huge primate tracks.

No oversized ape prints that day. Just wolf prints. There always were. Each morning I would wake up and climb out of my sleeping bag, suspended in a hammock ten feet above the ground. Every morning I found fresh wolf tracks encircling the tree, left by one or more lupine visitors chasing each other before pissing on the bark. As long as I hung my food in a bag, they rarely did anything to the non-edible parts of my campsite.

I returned to camp around dusk. I lit the fire and dumped a few cans of stew into a pot and set it on top of the grill to warm up. I know earlier I said to bring a lot of books, and you should, but you do develop a capacity to zone out for hours at a time in a way which is wholly impossible in a city. In a city you would hang yourself from boredom and loneliness, but those feelings are surprisingly moot in the wild. That said, you can also absorb yourself in a book and spend entire days thinking about it. Reading at dusk for me became a kind of mental dessert which capped off each day, and I looked forward to it tremendously. On this particular day, I looked forward to resuming *The Prince of Tides*. I wanted to finish a chapter before dark, and thought about it as I returned to my campsite.

The book was gone. I had set it right on top of my folding chair, and it was gone. "Dammit Bigfoot!" I yelled. I shook my fist at the tree line and jumped up and down. "You stupid, stinking ape-man! Fuck you, Sasquatch! Gimme my book back!"

By this point in time I'll admit I might have been starting to go a little crazy. If my mental stability were milk, for example, you would probably still drink it. But you would *think* about it first. Not clinical insanity, nor irreversible, just a tender loosening of my grip on reality. As I walked through the woods each day, Bigfoot's personality began to take shape in my mind. Bigfoot *was* there, intentionally evading my innocent research. Watching me from a distance, snickering at his effortless ability to thwart my reconnaissance. I personified the missing missing link in the same way certain people develop personal vendettas against fax machines or cars that won't start. So, without really thinking about the implausibility of the situation, I blamed Bigfoot for filching my book.

I stormed around the campsite, huffing and flipping things over, muttering and cussing. I have never handled losing my keys gracefully. I do the same thing even now, storming around my home, tearing things apart and cursing my own idiocy. Although I chanted "lousy Bigfoot" under my breath like a mantra, I mostly fumed at myself.

I ate my stew, sulking and casting evil glances towards the woods. "Very FUNNY, asshole!" I yelled, washing my bowl. "Yeah, you know what? *My* species has movable type! You might be able to steal a book, but we can *make* them. And we can bulldoze your precious forest, too! I'd like to see you hairy bastards wheel into one of our cities to knock the place down and plant saplings. Huh?" I did this a lot, insulting Bigfoot and then gloating over his inability to craft a witty retort. "Yeah, that's what I thought! Good night."

After brushing my teeth I heard the familiar howl of wolves in the distance. I only worried if they got *quiet*. Silence meant they were coming. I stared into the campfire and considered my situation. No evidence of Bigfoot. Ample evidence of wolves. Howling, tracks, ominous sense of death should I stay on the ground level beyond nine o'clock in the evening.

I fumbled through my back pack and found the bottle of sleeping pills. "For adults 12 years and over, take two pills. Do not exceed three in one twenty-four-hour period. Consult your doctor if you drink more than one alcoholic beverage per day." I imagined that two pills would conk a wolf out without killing it. Maybe the lupine equivalent of two and a half to three pills, assuming the creature wasn't a lush.

I whipped up a quick pot of oatmeal, broke the sleeping pills into a powder, and stirred them into the mash. I set the bowl next to the fire and whistled. "Here boy, here wolf!" A couple more calls, and I went to sleep, hoping to find a snoring red wolf next to my tree in the morning.

*

Dead raccoons lay everywhere. Everywhere. Ring-tailed carcasses scattered around the campfire. The morning after of a rodent doomsday cult which decided to don identical sneakers and join the mother ship.

"Dang," I said. I stood arms akimbo in front of the tree. I counted the unforeseen casualties of the otherwise brilliant plan. Seven. *Seven* dead raccoons. How could two measly sleeping pills kill so many animals? How could seven raccoons even go about sharing a bowl of oatmeal? Had I in fact been stalked by *fat racoons* these last two weeks, and not wolves at all?

I prepared my breakfast of toast with baked beans on top and considered my next course of action. *Probably best to just move on*, I thought. It was either that or dig a mass grave for the raccoons and hope I didn't inadvertently inter them in cursed Choctaw burial grounds. Simply not worth risking zombie rodents if my other option merely entailed relocating a hammock.

I spooned some more beans into my mouth using a piece of toast as a shovel, gazing out over the carnage. Raccoons look pretty cute when they've died of something other than automobile collisions. Like they're napping.

That's when a wolf ran out of the forest, ducked down to grab a dead raccoon by the neck, then darted away.

I blinked.

What?! I thought to myself. Had I just *seen* that? I counted the raccoon bodies. Yup. Down to six.

I washed and dried my plate and brewed a cup of coffee. The wolf's appearance indicated that my plan to drug it was viable, just lacking a few crucial steps. I somehow needed to turn "overdosed raccoons" into "healthy, comatose wolf."

I packed the tent and cooking gear up and tip-toed west through the raccoon corpses. An hour and a half later I re-established my base camp near Grampa's vineyard and cooked a healthy lunch of canned chili with stale Frito chips. I unfolded my chair and plopped down in it, shoveling spoonfuls of meat down my gullet and wondering what the overall sodium content of the canned goods I regularly consumed added up to.

As I scraped chili residue from the plastic bowl with my spoon, I spotted a wolf. Hesitant and quiet, observing me from a tree thirty yards away. Three weeks ago I would never have noticed, but woodland isolation heightens your senses. It's the tradeoff you get for all the new craziness.

I feigned ignorance. I opened a second can of chili and doled two more sleeping pills into its contents before setting the bowl down next to my folding chair. With minimal noise, I crept away and walked south for ten minutes. I took a break, I used the bathroom, then headed back.

The chili was gone. The wolf was unconscious. I was delighted.

Chapter 8

"A girl is a person who screams at the mouse and smiles at the wolf."

—Shyam Kapoor

I prodded the wolf with my foot to make sure it wasn't being clever. Nope. Out cold. A big, cinnamon-colored husky with a face reminiscent of a fox. I got a couple of bungee cords out of my backpack and bound its paws. Then I took a t-shirt and securely fastened the snout. It didn't budge. I hefted it over my shoulder and walked the fifteen-minute distance to Nashoba Vineyards, weaved through the rows of grapes, and slung the drugged wolf into the back of my Volvo.

I felt exhausted but exuberant as I opened the front door of Grampa's house and popped inside. "Grampa!" I yelled.

"What?!" he returned. I followed his voice to the dining room. He sat in a chair jotting ink from an old ballpoint pen onto parchment.

"What are you working on?" I asked.

"Prayers. Does your father have a mezuzah at the house?"

"I think so." I recalled at one point seeing a shiny doodad on our front doorjamb.

He nodded, but did not glance up from the tiny Hebrew characters. "This is the little scroll inside."

"I see." I walked over to the dining table and

looked down. Sure enough, Grampa was transcribing Hebrew characters onto the parchment. But that's all they were—characters. In the late eighties he struck onto the idea that certain Protestants might enjoy authenticating their religion by adding dashes of older Jewish spirituality on top. So he launched a successful side business producing and selling his own Hebrew prayers. Of course Grampa never actually *learned* Hebrew, but he did get his hands on a book of some sort, and dutifully memorized and copied his favorite undecipherable symbols onto exorbitantly expensive resume paper.

During the Gulf War a seminarian purchased one of Rabbi Heinrich's prayers and made quite a racket about the fact that they amounted to meaningless gibberish. The whole debacle culminated in a scathing editorial featured in *The Nambersaw Minuteman.* Prayer sales diminished considerably, but Grampa continued trickling out a few here and there as a sort of personal calligraphy hobby.

He blasted a stream of cigar smoke from his mouth onto the paper.

"Do people ever complain about the cigar smell?"

He glanced at me from beneath the Stetson's brim. "Just as soon as Virginia starts planting tobacco-frankincense hybrids, I'll flop over. Until then, it's all part of the magic. Did you find Bigfoot?"

"No," I said, beaming, "but I did capture a species of wolf previously thought extinct."

He shrugged. "Bravo. I don't suppose you're planning on keeping it, are you? Because I'm allergic to wolf."

"No, I've got it tied up in the back of my car. Do you have the phone number for Nambersaw's Animal Control Center?"

He looked at me quizzically. "In these parts 'animal control' is synonymous with the Second Amendment's 'right to bear arms.' If you're looking for some kind of government agency that doesn't shoot on sight, you'll need to head to McAlester."

"McAlester?" I balked.

He shrugged. "Your sweet old grandfather can instruct you on basic phone book usage if you need him to." He plugged the stogie back into his mouth and took a puff.

"No," I said, "I think I can figure it out." I forced myself to allocate some of the mirth from my bountiful wolf capture into our strained relationship.

"Glad to hear it. Will you be around for night-breakfast?"

"Yes, I think so."

"Good, I'm making Denver omelets. Be careful with that wolf, okay? To be honest with you, Saul, it strikes me as a terrible idea to bind a live wolf and transport it in the back of your Volvo. Have you ever had a cat get loose on the way to the vet? A wolf has got to be at least half that bad."

"Sure thing, Grampa. G'bye!"

I got into the car and drove away. It occurred to me that if I drove the hour and a half to McAlester to give up the wolf to Animal Control, I might not see it again. There could be complicated bureaucratic hoops to jump through. Hugo, on the other hand, took about as much time going south. And I had seen circus facilities there which could accommodate all sorts of species. I decided to head to Cindy's place and convince her to convince her father to lock the wolf up until I could determine and contact the proper scientific authorities.

After twenty minutes I called Cindy on my phone. "Hello?" Cindy asked.

"Cindy! I caught a wolf!"

"You what?" Static crackled across the line.

"I caught a *wolf!*"

"Sorry, Saul? I can't hear you."

"Hello? Cindy?" The connection cut out.

I drove another ten minutes and began to wonder how long the sleeping pills would last. In fact, I decided, it wouldn't be an altogether bad idea to relocate the wolf to my trunk. That way if it *did* regain consciousness, I wouldn't have to worry about it wiggling around.

I parked the car at a rest stop and popped the trunk, then removed the two bags of garbage from my camping excursion. I threw them in the rest stop's dumpster, like the responsible citizen I am, and returned to my car.

When I put my hand on the back door's handle, I froze. The wolf was gone. In its place, a snoring, thoroughly naked young woman lay sprawled out on my back seat. Pretty good looking, blonde-ish. Not a bad figure, albeit with most of the leg, armpit, and miscellaneous hair women usually remove. I stared at her for several moments in sheer disbelief. *What the hell just happened?*

A lot of things went through my mind, but the most prominent thought involved what exactly this might look like to a passing police officer. I imagined things would get complicated pretty quick. I guess I could claim she was my girlfriend and she was drunk, but of course I wouldn't. In the face of something so weird I would default to honesty, which would undoubtedly get me thrown in jail.

I quietly slipped into the driver's seat, the way you do when you're trying not to wake up an inexplicable naked person in your backseat. I lightly shut the door, fastening my seatbelt with the utmost candor. I turned the ignition, but did not shift the Volvo into drive. Where would I go? The wolf was gone. An inexplicable naked girl had taken its place.

Without any real plan, I headed back towards Nambersaw. I picked up my cell phone and checked the reception. Pretty good. I dialed Natalie.

Success! She picked up! "Natalie? It's Saul. Listen, I really need to talk to you."

"Is it important? I'm at work."

"There's a naked girl in my car."

Pause.

"Wow, you really play hardball with courtship, don't you?" Her voice grew loud and angry. "You know what, I talk to a guy all the time, and I don't bring that up around *you*. What kind of sick mind games—"

"Natalie, shut up! I don't know how she got here, okay!? One moment there's a drugged red wolf in my backseat, the next there's a naked girl." My mind frantically raked through its gray matter in search of a logical explanation. "Do you think she's an eco-terrorist?" I asked. "I got out of my car to throw some trash out, and when I came back the wolf escaped and this naked chick it in its place."

Yes, I thought, *this is actually sort of coming together now. Maybe she's with PETA or some other granola-loving acronym. Doing some sort of weird protest*

86

involving nudity. And it wouldn't surprise me if she was also high on drugs, of course, which would explain why she's passed out.

"I'm driving towards Lycan," I said.

"What?"

"Listen, I have *no idea* what to do here. Should I beat the police to the chase and drop her off at a station? Because—"

The naked girl sat up and started screaming. Then *I* started screaming. The cell phone clattered to the floorboards, which I stooped to pick up, still screaming, consequently steering the car off the road. I jerked up and continued screaming with the naked girl as I lurched the car back onto the pavement and hit the brakes, fishtailing the Volvo in a fit of squealing rubber.

The car stopped and we both slammed against our seat belts, gasping for breath. The naked girl clutched the seat in front of her, heaving back and forth.

"Okay," I said soothingly, "let's both just take a deep breath and—"

She started screaming again. A piercing wail which no doubt said "This man is a rapist and serial killer" to any passing automobiles.

"Calm down!" I shouted, prompting her to throw herself against the opposite window. She frantically fumbled against the panel before throwing the door open and tumbling out. She loped a few feet, looked back at me briefly in sheer, unblinking terror, then broke into a sprint towards the woods.

"Wait! Naked Girl!" I yelled. I grabbed my keys and gave chase. I do not know why.

"Naked Girl!" I called again. Orange, brown and

yellow leaves shot past me. I plunged through a tunnel of autumn in pursuit of the bounding, exposed skin. After a couple of minutes I lost track of her. I stopped to catch my breath, listening for the sounds of panicked footsteps on dry twigs and leaves. A crashing noise sounded off to my right, and I turned to follow it, dashing through an army of young elms which clawed at my face and shoulders.

I ran for five minutes straight, through and out of the forest, into a field. Finally, wheezing and exhausted, I bent over to catch my breath. The frightened nudist had escaped me. Odd, considering she didn't even have tennis shoes on.

I stood up to survey my surroundings and noticed leafy, shoulder-level greenery all around. I stepped forward and inspected the foliage. Marijuana. "Oh no," I said.

And that's when I heard the shotgun cock.

Chapter 9

"The timber wolves will be our friends
We'll stay up late and howl,
At the moon, till nighttime ends,
Before going on the prowl"

—Bill Waterson, *Calvin and Hobbes*

I turned around. Three men, all of whom looked very bored and tired, stared at me in an entirely menacing way. The one on the left was short and emaciated, with greasy hair and bloodshot eyes. The man in the middle had on ripped jeans and a yellowed undershirt. I don't remember what the man on the right wore, because I could only help looking at the sawed-off shotgun aimed at me, rhythmically swaying back and forth like a cobra.

"Lost?" The gunman offered, in an ominous monotone drawl.

"Yes," I said. "Yeah. I was. . . Well, that's not important. I was in the woods and inadvertently popped up here. In this alfalfa field." The gunmen spit out some tobacco and raised an eyebrow. "So, actually, you know what? I don't even need to cut through your alfalfa field. I'll just head back the way I came. *Through this alfalfa field.* Sorry to bother you." I turned around slowly and took a tentative step towards the woods.

"This is private property, slick. And you are trespassin'."

"Oh no," I said, laughing nervously, "just lost."

"Lost?" he asked. He looked to his companions expectantly. "That's a shame, *trespasser*. How bout we take you up to the house and give you directions?"

"Yeah," ripped-jeans guy offered. "Boss'd sure like to meet you, I 'spect."

I turned around and hazarded a goofy, don't-shoot-me grin. "Oh, I think I can find my way back, thanks."

The gunman sighed. "Slick, I've already cocked the gun once. I can't give you anymore non-verbal clues about yer situation. Mmkay?" I gulped and nodded. "Then why don't you walk with us back upta the house?"

"Yeah, that sounds good," I stammered, following them through the field of marijuana. I got nervous after a few seconds and began babbling in hopes of endearing them to me and thereby extending my life. "You guys ever watch *Field of Dreams*? Any baseball players wandering through here? Ha."

The gunman spat out some tobacco. "You sure are a chatty sumbitch."

We marched through the field of cannabis towards an old derelict homestead. A slumping, creaky farmhouse composed entirely of weathered shingles. Enough tinfoil covered the windows to satisfy the most paranoid of delusionals about warding off CIA surveillance. Accumulated rubbish pock-marked the grass: broken mason jars and an abundance of coffee filters with peculiar red stains. The place smelled like ammonia, like cat urine.

Yup, I thought, *this is a meth lab.*

The gunman gestured towards the door with the sawed-off. "After you, slick." I gulped and stepped inside. Cat urine, cat urine. Acetone and ether. I coughed, barely able to breath. Part of me worried that I might be inhaling carcinogens, but then I remembered I was far more likely to die from my irritating shotgun allergies in the next few minutes than succumb to disease at a later date.

The three men followed me inside and shut the door. I surveyed a disorderly living room with an attached kitchen. Empty beer cans and Doritos bags lay all over the carpet. "Take a seat," the gunman said, pointing at an orange, threadbare couch.

"Thanks!" I piped, lowering myself onto the cushions.

He turned to his associates. "When's Boss git back?"

The guy with ripped jeans shrugged. "Dunno, Chief. He's makin' a run to Little Rock, so prob'ly not fer awhile. Ten er 'leven?"

The gunman, "Chief," turned to me. "Looks like you might have to stay for dessert, too. Maybe even sleep over." He chuckled. "But I really doubt you'll stay *that* long."

"Ha ha!" I laughed, trying to bond with him through humor. *Shit I'm gonna die.* I could feel my heart rate accelerating, my blood uselessly sloshing through my arteries in a frustrated attempt to escape to safer locations.

Chief turned away from me. "Cookie?" he said.

"Yup?" the man with ripped jeans asked.

"Hows bout you getcherself to the garage and keep makin' them snacks?" Cookie nodded and exited the room. Chief pointed a thumb over his shoulder towards me. "If this *trespasser* tries anything funny, you comb his hair with this," he handed the shotgun to his cohort. "If you need me, I'll be in the shed."

"OkaysureChief!" the man blurted out. His eyes emphatically widened as he spoke, returning to slits when he stopped. Chief exited the house, leaving my captor to make himself comfortable on a stool in the kitchen, the sawed-off napping in his lap.

"So what's your name?" I asked.

His eyes bulged again. "MynameisStewartbutpeoplecallmeStu." The eyelids returned to half-mast.

"Uh-huh," I said, trying to keep calm. "You from around here?"

"Yeahjustuptheroadyourself?"

"Hoople, originally." Stu had greasy, brittle (is that possible?) hair. He was short and skinny, but his emaciated state seemed artificially-induced. Somehow, despite being thinner than me, he produced an aura of "fat kid." He snorted, then snapped away and furiously nibbled on his fingernails like a rabbit.

I wondered why these people bothered to black-out the windows. The place seemed pretty obvious. And it wouldn't take a police officer long to figure out that Stu dabbled in methamphetamines. I decided to avoid agitating him any further. He *seemed* harmless, sitting there gnawing on his cuticles. But who knew? He could snap at any moment and decide to blow my head off.

After a couple of minutes, he dropped his hand and stared at me with huge, dilated pupils. "Whoeryou?"

"Uh," I said. Did he honestly not remember he was supposed to be guarding me, or did he just mean my name? "Paul." If I managed to escape, leaving a pseudonym might be in my best interest. And "Paul" was close enough to my usual forename as to avoid confusing me.

"NicetomeetyouPaulIhopeIdontgottashootya."

"Thanks. Golly, me too! Nice to make your acquaintance."

"WhaddyadoforalivinthenPaul?"

"What?" I asked. Then, translating his speed-talking a moment later, I said, "I'm an anthropologist."

"Wazat?"

"Bigfoot hunter."

He grinned, revealing a row of teeth chemically peeled of any protective enamel. "YeretherelookinferBigfoot?"

I nodded. "Seen him?"

He grinned and bobbed on the stool excitedly. "YessirIdid! Twoweeksago!"

"Really?" I sat upright on the couch, affecting my most professional posture. "Care to tell me about it?"

I'm not entirely sure what he said. The excitement of telling the story accelerated his tempo beyond the usual pseudo ephedrine cantor. I'll paraphrase the conversation here as a halfway rational person might speak:

"A fortnight ago while stalking a gaggle of wild turkeys I intended to shoot I wandered through the very crop we discovered you in. I pursued the fowl to the nearby creek but lost track of them. That's when I realized that the creek was not water but

93

melted ice, or perhaps snow, and it also evaporates and is therefore part of the rain cycle, and that in a way we are *all* a part of this cycle, dying and decomposing and being reassembled in successor life forms and so forth, and I felt privileged to be a part of this great chain of being we call Life."

"Really?" I asked. (Keep in mind I'm paraphrasing this conversation.)

"Indeed. But that wasn't the point of my story. What were we talking about?"

"Your Sasquatch encounter."

"Ah yes! Well, after my epiphany that we are all interconnected, not just as life forms but on a sub-atomic level with rocks and the air and so forth, I crossed the creek bed and had a bowel movement next to a sapling. Between you and me, I suspect that I used poison ivy for the cleanup, with disastrous consequences. But that is only speculation, as I was slightly disoriented during the period in question for reasons which do not pertain to our current conversation. About. . . ?"

"Bigfoot."

"Of course, yes, Bigfoot. Once I finished relieving myself I caught sight of the turkeys again and followed them further down the creek bed in a general northeasterly direction, still intent on killing and eating one for dinner. And do you know what happened?"

"What?" I asked.

"What?" he countered.

"What happened?"

He squinted. "When?"

"When you were following the turkeys along the creek bed."

"Yes," he picked up, "I followed them and had a clear shot and I took my bead and—boom! The whole cosmos seemed to align with my hunting endeavors. I felt a cosmic connection with our hunter-gatherer forefathers, with the woodland predators, with the art of hunting. One shot and the turkey fell, deceased. Yet the turkey's mortality was not all that had changed. I *too* was altered by that epic gunshot."

"Uh-huh," I said. I patted myself on the back for not getting my hopes up about this meth head's Bigfoot sighting.

"For you see, when I stooped down to pick up my prize, I became cognizant of how flimsy mortality is. How delicate we all are. As I noted earlier, I arrived at a grand epiphany only minutes prior to this, that all life is one, and so how can you ever really detract or add to it? You cannot, I think, unless you obliterate the planet with nuclear warfare. Or desertification. That's why I do not flush toilets unless absolutely necessary—to stave off desertification. All the same, what are individual lives in this huge macro-organism? If life is a river, each organism is a bubble, popping and returning to that from whence it came. And I, a fellow bubble with fire power, had just popped another."

"That must have been hard on you."

"It was! It was!" he chortled. "But I'm getting away from the original point, aren't I? Perhaps some other time I'll share my observations from that fruitful week with you. Skipping ahead, I wandered onto someone else's field, and there I saw it. Erect in all its luminous beauty. *Could it be?* I thought. Surely not. Such a creature is mythical. But no! Verily, I saw it before me."

"Bigfoot," I said boredly.

"What?" He scrunched his face up. "No, a unicorn. Except that, when I drew closer, it turned out to be some kind of horse-like animal instead. Most likely a horse."

I slumped into the couch and yawned. "So you never actually saw Bigfoot, then?"

"Of course I did. Yesterday. I slept over at a friend's trailer and he walked by the front window around noon to deliver the mail. Which. . . you know, I think that might just have been the mail man?"

I nodded. "That was a wonderful story, Stu. Thank you." (I'll disengage the paraphrasing at this point.)

The door opened and Chief walked in. "Havin' fun, trespasser?"

"Just bonding with Stewart."

"You talk like a fag."

I forced a hard, brittle chuckle. "Nope, very heterosexual. Ha ha."

"Good." He pulled a joint out of his pocket and stuck it in his mouth. "Wanna a doobie?" He held one out to me.

I looked at the white cocoon in his palm. My sophomore year at Wily College I took a why-wade-when-you-can-jump philosophy to trying marijuana, by eating three edible Maui Wowie brownies. The experience did not much endear me to pot, although I briefly understood why people like Phish concerts and Led Zeplin, and it was interesting to see what it's like to be an inanimate object in between the monsoons of paranoia. I only got high twice after that, and both instances were purely because Cindy was at that time a Rastafarian and I was still unsuccessfully lobbying to get into her pants. By the time I graduated I decided I could get tired and hungry all by myself, thanks.

"Uh," I said. "Yeah, I'd love a doobie." I followed Chief outside and joined him in leaning against the rickety meth lab. Self-protection. If I toked up with him, it indicated I was no Boy Scout. We would be partaking of contraband communion, and I hoped that would somehow initiate me in his mind. He passed me a joint and lighter. I lit, inhaled, and coughed tremendously.

"How come you don't use a bong?" I asked, after regaining my composure.

"Yeah," he said, nearing conversational tones, "most folks like them better I guess. Smoother." He pulled another joint out of his pocket and scrutinized it. "Personally, I like rollin' 'em. When I was a kid I used to roll my own cigarettes, and I like rollin' too much to go buy some faggy glass pipe with polka dots and mushrooms all over it."

"Right," I said, trying with all my might to sound like I fit in. "Faggy bongs."

He finished his joint and popped the roach into his mouth and swallowed. "What's yer name?"

"Paul."

He nodded. "And why are you out here trespassin'?"

"The trespassing is entirely accidental," I said. I took another hit on the marijuana and felt my wits cool. Was this the last smoke before an execution? Well, better THC than nicotine if you want to take the edge off before your brains varnish the shingles, I

97

guess. "I was out in the woods doing anthropological studies."

He raised an eyebrow. "What's that?"

"Well basically," I said, smiling nervously, "I'm looking for Bigfoot."

He leaned against the shed and looked past me, out to the field. "That all?"

"That and only that," I said. Yes! Was he going to let me off the hook? Had I convinced him I wasn't a federal agent? "So far as I'm concerned, your farm is your business. I don't want to get involved."

"Glad to hear that. Well, were it up to me, Paul, I'd let you go. You seem okay. Definitely not from around here, kinda fruity, but not a fed 'er nothin'. But that's Boss's call, and he's not as lenient 's me."

The color drained from my face. "Listen, I don't want any trouble. If you let me go, I'll walk back through the woods. I don't even know where I am right now."

"No?" he said, eyebrows raised.

"No."

He smiled maliciously, turning back towards the house. "That was my next question—if anyone will know where to look for you. Gettin' cold out, aint it? Let's go back inside. Whaddya say?"

*

They provided dinner, which was nice of them, I guess. Hot dogs and stale bread with Taco Bueno hot sauce packets for condiments. I ate them gingerly with the warm, old Budweiser they offered, well aware it could be my last meal.

I'd like to say that I sat on that couch with

steely-eyed determination, staring down all of my would-be executioners, letting them know that I would hold my head high as I walked to the gallows.

But of course I didn't do that. I took deep breaths a lot, heaving a little, as if I'd just finished sobbing. I did everything in my power to shoot beams of "don't kill me" from my eyes like lasers. I thought, *You idiot. You had to go looking for Bigfoot. You idiot,* over and over again like a pessimist's rosary.

Stewart sat on an upturned paint bucket across from the couch, playing some deviant form of poker with Cookie and myself. We had spent the last hour playing the stupid game. I say "stupid" because the deck had two UNO cards and only three aces.

I constantly surveyed the room around me in sidelong glances, hoping to avoid suspicion. Did they lock the doors? I noted that one fourth of one window was missing aluminum foil. A tiny breach to the world beyond, although it was night out and made no difference. I checked for possible weapons. If left alone again, could I use something as a bludgeon? When would the aforementioned "Boss" turn up? How much longer did I have to live? I checked my watch. Seven o'clock.

"Got somewhere to be, slick?" Chief asked.

"Actually, yes," I said. "I told my grandfather I'd be home for breakfast by now."

"Breakfast?"

"Dinner," I corrected.

"Doyouwannacallhimonmyphonetolet'emknow you'llbelate?" blurted Stu, wide-eyed. He reached a grubby hand into one of his pockets but Cookie leaned over and slapped his phone to the floor.

"You can't let the trespasser make a *phone call*, Stu. We've been over this." Stewart nodded and ferociously chewed on a fingernail. That guy really did look like a huge man-bunny on drugs.

I glanced out the quarter-transparent window for the thousandth time. Except this time I saw a face. I couldn't see very well, but it looked like a girl staring in. I wouldn't say I winked at it, exactly, because "winking" implies some sort of playfulness. Let's say I terrifyingly half-blinked in her generation direction. *Natalie?* I thought. *Has she come to save me? Thank God!*

"Can I smoke in here?" I asked, reaching into a pocket.

"NO!" all three men responded. Which I was counting on: fumes.

"Okay, okay," I said. "Take it easy. Can I step outside for a sec, then?"

Chief squinted at me. "You're out there longer than a cig, and I'll feel compelled to make sure yer not lost."

I laughed. "Why would I stay out there any longer than I have to? Party's in here! Ha!" I stepped out of the trailer and put my hand in my pocket. "You guys want the door closed or open?"

"Open," Chief said.

"Sure, sure," I offered. I stepped away from the door and looked around. Where had Natalie gone? I silently but frantically gestured to the darkness for her to come my way. I pointed at the door and held a finger over my mouth.

A nude figure demurely stepped out behind a nearby tool shed. "Naked Girl?" I asked. I couldn't be sure it was the young woman from my car earlier, but it was certainly a stark-naked woman. Despite my imminent death and the implausibility of the situation, some mundane subroutine in my mind kept thinking, *She needs to put clothes on! It's getting cold out!*

She took a few cautious steps towards me. "He-hello?" she squeaked. What a nicely proportioned girl. Uplifting, shapely breasts. Muscular legs. I mentally slapped myself: how could my gonads possibly offer input at this time?

"Naked Girl!" I whispered. "You've got to get out of here! Go get help!" It occurred to me that she might be one of my wardens' girlfriends. That would account for the erratic, nudity-based behavioral deviance. "Do you know these guys?" I asked.

She shook her head. "I. . . no."

"Then go get help!" I hissed. But felt bad. She was naked. If she made it to a road, there was no guarantee a friendly trucker would squire her to a police station. Or that a car would pass by at all. Maybe someone would find her corpse the next day curled up in a fetal position beside the road, dead from exposure.

She took another step forward and wrinkled her nose. "It smells bad here."

"Yeah, that's the stench of volatile chemicals being superheated into crystal meth. Listen, before we devise an escape plan, can you tell me why you're naked?"

She looked lost and frightened. She could have communicated her expression through a full-length birka. She bit her lower lip and took a final step, stopping toe-to-toe in front of me. "I love you," she said, almost asked.

101

I gaped at her. Something within me snapped. Not lust, but intense, superhuman frustration. *"You love me?"* I hissed. "Love?!" My nostrils flared as I suppressed the urge to scream. "What the hell is wrong with your gender, huh?! Why do *all of you* instinctively start talking about love and commitment as soon as you're naked around me? I'm being held hostage by meth heads and you want to talk about *feelings?"*

She rocked back from the emotional outburst. Then, after a moment of deliberation, lunged forward to kiss me, knocking our teeth together with the force of the blow. I struggled briefly, then melted into the embrace. She grabbed my ass with her hand, grinding us together, radiating heat out from the contact spot. I ran a hand through the hair at the base of her neck, then yanked it away. I pushed her slightly and took a breath of air.

"Listen, Naked Girl," I said, dropping my gaze to afford her maximum eye-contact. "I'm all about hooking up with you, okay? But we're going to get shot if you don't disappear, now. GO GET HELP." I lightly pressed my palms against her collar bone to nudge her back. She pulled it down to her breast. "Go!" I whispered, reluctantly pulling back.

I heard footsteps behind us. Stewart walked out from the house a little ways and unzipped his pants. "Aaaaaaah," he said, putting his hands behind his head in a free-style urination pose. He gave himself a shake, zipped up and turned to face me, head bent in an effort to light the joint in his mouth. The lighter sparked several times but failed to ignite a flame, so he chucked it into the field. "HeyPaulyougotanymatches?" He nodded politely to Naked Girl. "Miss," he said.

"What?" I asked. I glanced at the girl who had, moments earlier, confessed her love to me. "No, I'm all out. I could. . . Do you want me to get a lighter for you from inside?"

He grinned, exposing cores of teeth, hideous even in the dark. "Nahthat'sokayI'llgogetalightfromChief." He cackled, wheezing an invisible cloud of ammonia-scented fumes our way. He slapped a hand on my shoulder and turned around. "Okay. Seeyouinaminute. Say," he said, his speed momentarily disengaging to normal levels, "do you wanna play Monopoly? Because the guys say the game takes too long, but I think it's *worth* it."

"Sure," I said. "I love Monopoly. Can I be the top hat?"

"Ha! You *wish!* But you can be the dog."

"The dog was my second choice."

"Okie-doke." He walked back to the door, then paused. His hands dropped to his sides. He turned around and stared at us with the expression of a man working out a complicated dinner tip in his head. "Izzere anakedgirl nexcha?"

I glanced at my bare-ass companion. "Nope," I said. "Just me."

"Okiethen." He stepped into the house, then, seconds later, walked backwards out of it. He pointed at me and snapped, grinning. "Nicetry! Heyguys!" he yelled. "There'sahotnakedgirloutside! Guys! C'mere!"

"Run!" I yelled, grabbing Naked Girl's hand. "Run!"

*

I heard the sawed-off erupt from behind us. "Don't shoot *her!*" screamed Cookie. "Just Paul! Kill *Paul!*"

We bounded into the field of marijuana, thankfully up to our shoulders in height. "Duck!" I shouted, releasing Naked Girl's hand and bending over. She dropped to all fours, and without any deceleration continued to career through the field of cannabis. Flashlights zipped over the tops of the stalks. A second shotgun blast rocked nearby vegetation.

I went down on all fours, veering off from Naked Girl's trajectory. "Paul!" shouted Chief. "Paul, stand up! We just want to talk to you!" *Blam!*

I ran a hand through my hair. This was it. Make or break, run or croak. I shuffled on all limbs, scraping my palms and knees and feeling blood squirt between my fingers. If I could only get to the edge, to the woods—I could lose them in the woods. Safety was only a forest away.

I sprinted again, whipping stalks of cannabis against my face, then stopped to catch my breath. I forced myself to take long, quieter intakes of air, listening for approaching gunmen. I heard shouting behind me towards the meth lab. Then gunfire, this time from a rifle, and more shouting. Why weren't they combing the field for us? Had Naked Girl gone back that way, trying to find me?

Behind me I could hear yelling, frantic in its pitch and volume. Multiple salvos of ammunition thundering through the night. What on earth was happening? I turned around and crouched, then ever so carefully raised my eye level above the stalks.

At the farmhouse I could make out Chief, Cookie and Stewart standing on the porch, waving their guns erratically. Blood poured down Chief's face, forcing him to constantly reach up and wipe his eyes with a sleeve. A nasty gash ran the length of Cookie's leg. Stewart fired his rifle, nearly tipping over from the kick back.

Then I saw them: wolves. Three or four, circling the meth lab, weaving in and out of the marijuana. My former captives were unsuccessfully trying to get a bead on them. Chief fired again, and missed. "Dammit!" he swore. "You fucking coyotes!" He cocked the sawed-off and ineffectively blasted a nearby stalk of marijuana.

A wolf shot out from the brush, zipping past them, into the weeds on the other side. Chief swiveled to fire at the beast, then pulled the trigger. He caught Cookie in the arm with a spray of shotgun pellets, lacerating the flesh in violent mist of blood. Cookie dropped his gun and screamed, clutching the mess of wounds extending from his shoulder to his elbow. "Inside! NOW!" yelled Chief.

He grabbed Cookie by the good arm and lugged him into the derelict farmhouse. Stewart barreled after them, but a wolf dug into his leg and nearly pulled him into the field. He fell over and fired his rifle, sending the animal yelping and limping into the vegetation.

Stewart crawled on his elbows into the farmhouse, kicking the door shut behind him. From within, Chief ripped the aluminum foil off the windows and thrust his sawed-off through a pane of glass. He fired a shot indiscriminately towards the marijuana, then tilted it to aim directly in front of the door. Behind him, the lights flickered on. Stewart shattered another window as he ran his rifle through the pane.

For a few moments everything stood tense and silent. Until the lights went off. I heard muffled screaming from the farmhouse. The sawed-off and rifle pulled back from the window. Inside, the darkened house lit with bursts of light from the men frantically firing their weapons, screaming over the barking and growls.

Then everything got quiet.

I stood in the field, jaw agape. *I need to get out of here. I need to climb a tree, get to safety from the wolves,* I thought.

I turned around to go, but saw the door to the farmhouse swing open from the corner of my eye. A man lurched out, but not one of the embattled meth men: Arno Phenris. Naked, with blood dripping from mouth and running down his neck. Two wolves brushed past his legs and then disappeared into the night.

Arno sloped off the porch with a bottle in his hand and lit a rag sprouting from the neck. The cloth ignited, soaked in kerosene or another flammable liquid. He walked further away from the farm house and chucked the Molotov cocktail at its roof.

The fire spread with gusto. It only took a few seconds before the fumes inside ignited, and the house exploded as I imagine a small microwave would when put inside of a larger microwave.

The force of the blow knocked Phenris over. He stood up, brushed himself off, and walked towards the field. Smiling, covered in blood. The fires of hell blazing behind him.

Chapter 10

"There are, of course, several things in Ontario that are more dangerous than wolves. For instance, the stepladder."

—J.W. Curran
The Canadian Wildlife Almanac, 1981

Never before in my life had I been so deserving and desirous of hard liquor. A naked girl. A near-death experience at the hands of tweekers. Ferocious wolves. And the eerie paranoia which accompanies questioning your own sanity—when you begin to openly speculate about werewolves.

I frantically pondered this possibility as I drove back towards Nambersaw. I knew that, at the very least, Arno Phenris seemed to get a kick out of killing people. While naked. But the creatures terrorizing my meth head captors were *wolves*. And the creature which I had captured and put in my car had been a wolf, not a naked blonde girl. I felt very confident about this—I had *definitely* not captured a naked woman and tied her up in the back of my car. You remember that sort of thing.

"Werewolves," I said to myself. "I do believe I'll have a drink."

I bypassed Grampa's house entirely and instead drove into Nambersaw proper to lubricate my aching brain lobes at a favored watering hole named Former's. Called such because of its previous incarnation as the Nambersaw Synagogue.

Grampa purchased the building from a group of Quakers in 1950, and it still looks a little like a church from the outside. The steeple has been removed, but its exterior maintains the red-brick church decorum partial to small town ministers, despite the flashing neon beer advertisements along its windows.

I stepped inside and took in the tavern. Notwithstanding the vaulted ceiling and enormous windows, the place felt sordid and cave-like. Permanent clouds of smoke bounced off the stained brick walls like dimwitted cirrus clouds. Sporadic yellow light bulbs cast a seedy glow on the tables, throwing ghoulish cowboy shadows on the floor. The former synagogue's religious iconography had been removed years ago, but a couple of pews still leaned against the wall as a throwback to the location's earlier days. A bearded man in ostrich boots lay passed out on one; a panting, groping couple got to know each other on the other.

Former's retained a few splashes of zest. The pool tables near the back were well lit, and the nearby jute box tumbled out frothy Western songs. Festive bottles, spirits and the entire selection of Nashoba Vineyard's products lined the shelves behind the bar. Miraculously, the three elements elevated the place from a hole-in-the-wall to a comical, self-aware hole-in-the-wall. It's the sort of place hipsters, when they later became a cultural force, might call "authentic." Although the intermittent bar fights would surely scare off any well-coiffed men in smirky jeans looking to colonize such an establishment.

Former's is the Plymouth Rock of my family.

Were it not for it and the vineyard, the Heinrichs would never have become Jewish. Grampa would not be the progenitor and patriarch of our family, but a branch in a larger tree. All thanks to Prohibition.

Although Grampa was already four years old by the time the United States ratified the Twenty-First Amendment, Oklahoma doggedly continued prohibition until 1959. The state's puritanical resolve allowed Grampa to develop a knack for bootlegging years after the rest of the country had moved on to legally enjoying liquor.

His future father-in-law, John Black Kettle, established Nashoba Vineyards the year Congress repealed federal prohibition. He was a full-blooded Choctaw, and by virtue of this was able to claim the vineyard as part of the Choctaw Nation and therefore not subject to the state law of Oklahoma. When Grampa, a white man, inherited the vineyard by marrying John Black Kettle's daughter, the vineyard lost the Indian legal impunity under which it had previously found protection. By all rights the vines should have been dug up and the land converted to pasture. But Grampa, quite the entrepreneur, was thrilled at the prospects of adding alcohol production to his existing bootlegger portfolio, and disinclined to let teetotaler mandates curtail his enterprise.

One loophole to these ridiculous liquor regulations allowed for alcohol used in conjunction with religious ceremonies. Catholics, for instance, absolutely insisted on using wine instead of grape juice for communion. The state grudgingly allowed them the practice. But Catholics were highly suspect in those times, and Grampa believed it would hurt business to become a papist. Jews, however, weren't even on the radar in Oklahoma. And he stumbled onto an article somewhere stating that they used sweet wines in many of their services.

Thus, in 1950 Gunther Heinrich declared himself a Jewish rabbi. His father, who had come to Nambersaw explicitly to scare Christ into the debauched former mining town, never spoke to him again. Nor did any other existent member of the Heinrich clan.

Gunther proceeded to blindly create his own religion in a part of the country where no one could call him out on it. He penned hymns extolling glorious episodes of Moses outwitting Harry Bradford, the nemesis farmer who lived down the road. He concocted scripture about golems devouring children too lazy to go grape picking.

Grampa operated Nashoba Vineyards as a supplier of ceremonial Jewish wines, simultaneously opening the Nambersaw Synagogue as a thinly-veiled speakeasy. It is for this reason, combined with Grampa's flamboyantly dishonest business practices, that "Antisemitism" in Oklahoma was for much of the twentieth century only a statement of hating my family.

The bizarre thing is that, when the state reluctantly lifted its ban on liquor in 1959, Grampa *remained* Jewish. By then he had fashioned a rabbinical identity. He had reared his children as devout followers of his outlandish, homemade religion, and saw no reason at all to give it up. It made little difference to him that his Torah was assembled from plagiarized Farmer's Almanac maxims. By his reasoning the fact that he had made

111

up his creed did not make it any less viable.

The beer hall in which I stood was the singular monument to his deviant religion. For years Grampa had presided over Shabbat here, a necessary religious service visitors participated in before the "ceremonial bibbing" which extended to all hours of the night. The "hymns" which my family inexplicably maintains were fashioned here: dirty cowboy songs which Grampa slightly altered the lyrics of to create his own Hebrew hymnal.

I sat down at the bar and waited for someone to take my order. I noticed a black-and-white photograph hanging near the door. It featured a young Rabbi Heinrich in the center of a pew, surrounded by grinning and flushed men in suits. The caption read: "Rabbi Heinrich and the Women's Temperance Society's Husbands, 1953."

Below it hung a sepia tone picture of Grampa with several bleary-eyed state legislators and a blottoed general. Each politician barely held a wine glass. Although the forerunners of Friends in Merlot Places and Tipsy Golem were always popular drinks, originally the most fashionable beverage was a victual called Talmudic Rocket Fuel, which Grampa reluctantly discontinued in the mid-sixties after a ranch hand drank too much and paralyzed himself by falling off a step-ladder. The general in the photograph loosely gripped a mug in his right hand, which probably contained Talmudic Rocket Fuel judging by the Tower of Pisa angle he stood at.

A woman sauntered over to me before stepping back in amazement. "Saul?"

I nodded, smiling. "Hey, Aunt Betsy." She looked like the essence of lunch lady, distilled and amplified into a hulking bartender. A big-boned, makeupless, cut-the-crap woman. Amos's ex-wife and current proprietor of Former's. Not that she won the bar through the circus festivities accompanying their divorce. Nope, Amos lost his birthright to her at a cock fight.

She punched me in the shoulder and grinned. "Are you of age now?" I nodded. "Thought so. What'll it be? First drink's on the house."

"What kind of beer do you have?"

She looked back at the selection on the wall. "Cold."

"My favorite! I'll take that and two shots of whiskey. I have a lot of thinking to do."

Aunt Betsy poured me two shots of amber rot gut from a plastic bottle under the sink. "Free of charge, Saul. You want a napkin and a pen to help you reason things out?"

"No," I said. "I might talk to Uncle Amos if he's around, though. Is he here?"

Betsy grimaced. "Of course he is. There's only one bar in Nambersaw, isn't there?" It was true. A county law prohibited the sale of liquor within so many feet of churches or schools. As Nambersaw had almost as many churches as people, sometimes more, only one triangular shaped plot in the entire municipality could theoretically sell anything stronger than Pepsi. A little island sanctuary of booze dominated by Former's. She handed me my beer and pointed to a booth in the corner. "Your toad of an uncle is over there."

"Thanks," I said, unseating myself from the stool. Amos's figure filled the booth like a stack of tires with a cowboy hat perched on top. He propped up his hulking torso against the tabletop with his elbows, one hand clutching a personalized mug. Which is to say, a glass mug with "AMOS" scratched into it with a switchblade.

I slid across from him in the booth and took a sip of my beer. "I admire you being able to work through your bitter divorce in order to continue drinking here."

He grunted amicably and took a gulp of lager. "And what brings you here, Sauly? Finally get yourself a divorce as well?"

"No," I said. "I just escaped the clutches of a bunch of narcotic-sucking hillbillies, who were in turn devoured by wolves. But if you want to commiserate about women, I can do that."

Amos leaned back in his seat, making the booth creak in protest. "I'm not drinking because of your Aunt Betsy, Saul."

"Then why *are* you drinking?"

He took a gulp of beer and smacked his lips. "Inertia." Amos sucked down the last of his beer, then pointed at my mug and snapped until I downed it. "Betsheeba!" he yelled.

"What?!" Betsy screamed back from the bar.

"Bring us a damn pitcher of beer!"

"In a damn minute!" Amos stared at the residual bubbles in his personalized mug until she delivered the pitcher.

"Thanks, ex-sugar. Can you put it on my tab?"

"You haven't paid your tab in two weeks, ex-honey."

"Okay, how about *I used to own this bar!*" He slammed his mug onto the counter, making nearby coasters hop.

Betsy harrumphed. "If you don't pay up by the end of the week, I'm cutting you off."

Amos winked at her. "You're just as beautiful as the first day of our separation, former darlin'." He topped up our drinks as she retreated to the bar. "Care to go to a cock fight with me this weekend?"

"No thanks," I said. I took a gulp.

Amos grew suddenly serious. "So the wolves came after you?"

"Not tonight, no. They came after the meth heads who captured me."

He reacted stoically, seemingly unmoved by my brush with death. My experience had only made one of his own troubling memories resurface, which may or may not have been related to Aunt Betsy. "Be careful out there, Saul."

"Didn't you say you saw something once, Amos?" I asked.

He nodded. "Yes."

I looked at him expectantly. "Can you share it with me?"

He pursed his lips and drummed pudgy fingers on the table. "Alright," he said slowly. "Finish your poison. There's a good man. But I don't want you quoting me in your project, okay?"

"Not a problem."

He pulled a pocket knife out of his jeans and absently whittled designs on his mug. "About eight years ago I was hunting deer in the Quachitas."

"Isn't that a national forest preserve?"

He nodded. "And it wasn't deer season, either. That's half the reason I don't want my name showing up anywhere."

"I see."

115

"I had set up a deer blind in the woods, and been out there for about… three hours, I guess. And this," he shuddered, "this *thing* came out of the trees. Just for a second. Hunched over but on its hind legs, maybe five feet tall. Whatever it was, it wasn't human. Too much hair." Goosebumps rose on his forearms. "It *looked* at me," he said, pointing to his eyes. "And," he leaned forward and dropped his voice, "I could swear it *smiled* at me, Solomon. Then it was gone."

He shuddered again and leaned back in his chair. "Needless to say, I got the hell out of there. I slept with my rifle by the bed for three weeks after that. With the curtains pulled and a light on."

"That's astounding," I said, getting excited. "Tonight I saw a man with the wolves, who—"

"That's not the end of the story, Saul. The next day they found a hunter in the woods. Now, the *papers* say he was older and succumbed to hypothermia. But I'm buddies with some of the rangers out there. Specifically the one who found his body."

"What was his version?"

Amos leaned forward and stared at me. "They found the man with his throat ripped out. In his car. One of the windows was broken, with claw marks up and down the door." He leaned back and finished his beer. "I don't know why the authorities made up the story about hypothermia. But I saw the expression on the ranger's face when he told me about it. Keep drinking."

"That's," I said, feeling a little uneasy. "That's an amazing story."

Amos nodded. "So that's my word of wisdom to

you, nephew. Remember that if you go out monster hunting, you might actually *find* a monster."

I finished my beer and poured a sequel. "I think I did, Amos." We stared at each other apprehensively. He refilled his beer and held his mug aloft in a silent salute, then downed it.

"A werewolf," he said. I nodded. He sat quietly, contemplating this for some time. "I believe you."

"But, but Amos—that's *crazy*, right?"

He smiled. "Sure is. You wanna fill me in on the details?"

I explained the captured wolf, the inexplicable naked girl, my capture, and Arno Phenris.

Amos whistled. "Shit! Sounds like there's a whole *tribe* of the damn things. I always figured there was just one."

"So you thought the monster you saw was a werewolf?" I asked.

He swirled his beer around before nodding. "I suppose I tried not to think about it much, Saul. But yes. You spend enough time deer hunting by yourself, or listening to local barflies shoot the shit, and you realize there's a lot of details floating around that don't really fit in with reality that well. And it sure seems crazy the *first* time you think it, but then you start looking around and remember that everyone in town believes in angels and miracles and virgin births, and then you start to think, who knows, maybe if some of the crazy stuff is real some of the other crazy stuff is, too. Maybe the dark stuff."

I leaned forward to grasp Amos's hand. "Amos, I saw men killed today. Killed by wolves—by a werewolf. What do we do?"

Amos shrugged. "I don't know, Saul. But I'll tell

117

you another thing. I think your Grampa knows about the wolves, too." He leaned forward and dropped his voice to a whisper. "I think he's got an agreement with 'em."

Chapter 11

"Little Red Ridin' Hood
I'd like to hold you if I could
But you might think I'm a big bad wolf so I won't"

—Ronald Blackwell, "Lil' Red Riding Hood"

I woke up the next day at eleven, coughing. From cigar smoke. My eyes fluttered open and I screamed, because Grampa Rabbi was sitting at the foot of the bed watching me sleep. "What the hell are you doing?!" I demanded. I sat up in bed, pulling my feet away from him. He shrugged. "Creepy! Creepy, Grampa!"

He smiled and blew a puff of cigar smoke at me. "How did the wolf relocation go?" His eyes glinted.

I harrumphed. "How do you think?"

"Pretty good I suppose, considering you're not dead."

I batted at a tendril of smoke. "It got away."

"That so? Well, as you no longer have a hell hound to wrangle, perhaps you can lend yourself to some wine-related labor this afternoon?" I groaned. Grampa tut-tutted. "Free room and board, and you can't even help an old man on a work project?"

"Fine," I said. "That's fine."

He patted my foot through the quilt. "Good boy." He swapped another ten minutes of his life for a long drag on the cigar and expelled it through his nostrils like a dragon. "I thought you might like

119

breakfast in bed."

I rubbed my eyes. "Sure, that sounds good." My head hurt.

He nodded and stooped over, returning to an upright position to lob a box of waffles at me. "Frozen waffles?" I asked, catching them before they hit me in the face.

"Don't worry," Grampa said, bending over. He stood up and chucked a toaster onto the bed, which nearly bounced onto my groin. "Syrup?" he asked, withdrawing a travel-size bottle of maple syrup from his trousers.

"No thanks. That seems unnecessarily complicated."

Grampa smiled. "Smart lad. Nobody likes sticky sheets."

He placidly watched me breathing, for an uncomfortable amount of time. I dimly returned his gaze, wondering if he were trying to initiate some kind of awkward staring contest. "Do—"

"I've got another brilliant idea," he said. Grampa liked to introduce his epiphanies by interrupting people mid-conversation. To illustrate their relative importance.

"What's that?"

"I was rifling through an old copy of *Scientific American* yesterday, and I found an article on music and plants."

I raised my eyebrows and nodded, beckoning him on. He stared at me. "What—"

"Basically," he continued, "plants *enjoy* classical music. They grow better."

"Uh," I said.

"I went through some gardening magazines,

and they said the *same thing*. House plants grow better if you put them near a radio and put on classical music."

"That doesn't make—"

"So this morning I went into Nambersaw and bought four hundred dollars' worth of audio speaker equipment. We're gonna rig 'em up throughout the vineyard, like music sprinklers. Vivaldi," he added proudly. "*Four Seasons*."

"Just so I'm clear on this, we're going to pipe baroque music over a speaker system for the benefit of your grape vines?"

He nodded furiously. "I think I'm onto something here, Saul. Apparently, it's a standard trick with home gardeners. But nobody's ever even thought of exposing *crops* to classical music!" He threw up his hands, which vibrated in geriatric excitement. "Not even Bordeaux does it. Just dead silence, and maybe a little French now and then. We're gonna be cutting-edge, m' boy." He squinted at the ceiling, as if reading its contours like tea leaves. "'Nashoba Vineyards: The *Smartest* Wine on Earth!'"

"Uh-huh," I said.

He winked and exited the room, leaving an orphaned fug of cigar smoke to dissipate in his wake. I leaned over and plugged the toaster into a wall socket, jamming a couple of Eggo's into its slots. I waited only long enough for them to thaw before cramming the soggy, luke-warm disks into my mouth. I downed a maple syrup chaser right out of the bottle. My phone rang. Natalie.

"Saul, are you alright?" She sounded genuinely concerned.

"I'm fine," I said. "Not hungover at all."

121

"That's. . . yes, good, that's why I was calling. Nothing happened when you got home?"

"The old man's too feeble to beat me, if that's what you're worried about."

"Is he okay?"

"Yes," I asked. "Did I miss a tornado or something? Why all the concern?"

"Do you remember any of the text messages you sent me last night?"

I furrowed my brow. "I sent you text messages?"

"Several. The ones that didn't involve my 'epic rack' mentioned something about you meeting some combination of rednecks and wild animals?"

"Hold on a sec." I thumbed through my mobile phone's outgoing texts. They were myriad.

TO: NATALIE, 10:43 PM.

HAVE YOU HEARD THAT SAYING ABOUT THE CHAOS THEORY, THAT WHEN A BUTTERFLY FLAPS ITS WINGS A TSUNAMI HAPPENS IN ASIA? I BET WHEN YOUR BREASTS SHIFT WHOLE CITIES ARE LEVELED BY EARTHQUAKES.

I grimaced and scrolled on.

TO: NATALIE, 11:07 PM

DID WE SPEND HUNDREDS OF YEARS BREEDING BEAGLES INTO FAT BASSET HOUNDS? WHY DID WE DO THAT? WERE THEY

GETTING TOO FAST?

"I'm sorry," I said. "I feel like an idiot."
"Keep reading."

TO: NATALIE, 11:12 PM

YOU ARE SO PRETTY AND SO
SMART! I KNOW WE'RE JUST
FRIENDS BUT WE SHOULD GO
OUT ON A DATE SOMETIME
ANYWAY. LIKE ROMANTICALLY.
ALSO, IF I EVER BECOME
SURGEON GENERAL, I WILL
SPEND A LOT OF TIME YELLING AT
PEOPLE WITH A BULLHORN,
ORDERING THEM TO JOG.

"This is awful. I'm so sorry," I said, turning
crimson. I dimly recalled Amos and I finished off a
fourth pitcher of beer, long after we'd abandoned the
weighty subject of werewolves.
"You sent twenty or thirty messages like that.
Look later in the evening, just before you called me."
"Okay."

TO: NATALIE, 11:48 PM

DUCK-BILLED PLATYPUSES:
HOAX? VERY.

TO: NATALIE, 11:52 PM

THEY SAY IT'S HALF AND HALF,
BUT WHAT IS THE HALF THAT'S

123

NOT MILK???

TO: NATALIE, 11:59 PM

IN VALHALLA THERE IS ONLY
LAUGHTER AND BLUEGRASS.

TO: NATALIE, 12:30 AM

WINDOWS ARE JUST WALLS THAT
LACK WILL POWER.

"Some of these are at least kind of cute, right?" I
said. "I mean, isn't it a nice gesture that I took the
time to text you so much? The one about windows
sounds like a Buddhist koan."

"Some of them were funny. But if I hadn't
already got to know your 'sense of humor' the last
month I would have called the cops and buried my
phone in the backyard. Check your messages around
a quarter to one."

TO: NATALIE, 12:41 AM.

I NEARLY DIED TODAY. STUPID
REDNECKS. STUPID WOLVES.
MONSTERS! THERE ARE
MONSTERS NATALIE! MONSTERS
ARE REAL!

TO: NATALIE, 12:42 AM

DO YOU THINK WED FIT OKAY
GIVEN THAT YOURE A HEAD

"Oh, right," I said, returning to the receiver. "Yes, I was captured by meth heads, but wolves devoured them. Which is neat, sort of, because it means the various things trying to kill me are cancelling each other out."

"It's the circle of life," she said. "What are you doing tonight?"

I fell on my back and looked up at the ceiling. I could not recall if Amos and I had cobbled together a reasonable werewolf prevention plan. I doubted it. I felt exhausted and hungover and ill-equipped to deal with a monster infestation.

"Packing?" I said. "I'm pulling the plug on my Bigfoot research, Nat. I haven't found a single footprint or hair, and the only Sasquatch stories I've heard are from my uncle regarding his ex-wife. Fruitless anthropology isn't worth getting eaten in the woods over. I'm leaving."

"You're. . . can I give you a sendoff? I'll buy you a drink at that bar in Nambersaw. Or you can come over for dinner."

I contemplated this. I liked Natalie. A lot. But my enthusiasm was scattered across the linens and soggy waffle crumbs. There were bound to be other hot girls in less debilitating locations. "No, I don't really feel like going out. I'll be here at the vineyard."

"I could bring a movie over," she offered.

"Grampa doesn't own a DVD player. He has a VCR, but only to hide flasks in. Although apparently he owns a good deal of audio equipment."

"Oh."

"You can still come over, though. I'll make us. .

." I trailed off before saying "breakfast." Best to ease her into Heinrich family insanity. "Do you like sausage? We have a lot of sausage. And how about some fruit-topped Belgian waffles for desert?"

"That's sounds delicious!" A smile broke on the other end. "I'll see you around seven?"

"Grand," I said, and joined Grampa in the winery.

*

Natalie showed up at eight, but she looked gorgeous so I skipped the lecture about punctuality I'd been preparing. Her hair was wavy, almost curly, with its ends bouncing on a tight gray turtle-neck. A Valkyrie in cowboy boots.

"Hi!" I said. "Come in. Are you hungry?" I hung her crimson Vanderbilt hoody on the coat hanger and gave her a hug. She wrapped her arms around me and squeezed, lingering a tantalizing moment longer than necessary. "I had dinner with my parents, but there's always room for Belgian waffles."

"Right." She followed me into the kitchen. "Would you grab whatever fruit you want out of the refrigerator and wash it out?"

"Sure," she said. Did she smell like lilacs? Was that for my benefit? Had to be. Or maybe she always cleaned up like that to counter-balance ranch stench. "So," she said, "I'm mostly here to learn about your brush with death. And to persuade you from leaving. Where do you want to start?"

"With food. I'll explain as we eat. Would you like any wine?"

126

I opened a cabinet to reveal Grampa's current stock. She stared at it and made a contemplative humming noise. "What would you suggest? What kind of wine compliments waffles?"

"Pinot noir," I said. "Definitely pinot." I uncorked the bottle and poured us each a glass. A couple of minutes later I set them and the Belgian waffles on the dining room table.

Natalie nibbled on a piece and smiled at me. I smiled back, but I felt awful. She looked gorgeous smiling. Were my pupils dilating? Oh, this was terrible. Most of my feelings for her had previously been caught up in a marvelous middle school crush. And those types of crushes are wonderful. They involve adoring a pretty girl and sighing when she leaves the room, then rapidly forgetting her and moving onto other subjects. They're terrific for when you're living by yourself in the woods.

Across from her now, I could sense my feelings had matured into a full-blown tossing-and-turning-in-bed-at-night adult infatuation. In another day or two I would return to civilization as an unemployed, failed Bigfoot hunter, and have nothing to think about, *nothing*, except the corners of her mouth pulled up in a playful smirk. Those brown irises that turned green around the edges like emerald coronas. Looking for a means of feeding myself would be a welcomed distraction.

"So. Death," she prompted.

For the next five minutes she listened to me explain the previous night's proceeds, jaw agape, a cool square of Belgian waffle hovering from a fork two inches from her mouth. When I finished she set it down. "Saul, I'm so glad you're okay. I. . . I

127

thought you might have been in a car wreck or something, not avoiding gunfire and wild animals and explosions."

"Thanks," I said. I took a deep breath and prepared to launch into my story's crazy conclusion, involving a naked and blood-smeared Arno Phenris, but stopped as Grampa entered the kitchen humming Vivaldi's *La Primavera*. "Solomon," he chided, "where's your kipah?"

I swiveled around and glared at him. "Grampa, I have," I almost said "a friend," but was afraid the acknowledgment would harden our otherwise ambiguous platonic status. "I have company over!"

He glanced at Natalie and smiled. "And what lovely company at that." He sauntered to the dining table and sat across from Natalie, eye-twinkling kicked up to Mach 4. "And what's your name, my dear?"

"Natalie Rougarou," she said, extending a hand. He kissed it, looking up at her through toothbrush bristle eyebrows. "I'm Rabbi Heinrich, Solomon's grandfather." He leaned back and put his hands behind his head, in a look of supreme self-satisfaction. "So what's your favorite thing about me?"

Natalie smiled. "Love the cowboy hat."

I glared at the old man. *Stop!* I thought, hoping he might catch a whiff of my brainwaves. It's not that he had a chance with Natalie, even a little bit. I just didn't want him showing me up in the charm department. And for his many foibles, Grampa *did* reek of charm. He was sopping wet with charisma.

He pulled a cigar out and clamped it between his lips. Bony fingers reached into his black suit to withdraw a matchbook. Seconds later a volcanic cloud of nicotine rolled through the air.

"Grampa, we have company," I growled.

"Oh!" he said, snapping to attention. "Where are my manners?" He reached into his pocket and pulled out a long, skinny cigar. "Here you are, darling," he said, holding it out to her between his bony middle and index fingers.

I balked. "That's not—"

"Thanks!" Natalie laughed and took the cigar, gripping it between her fingers in what I imagined was an attempt to pose as Audrey Hepburn in *Breakfast at Tiffany's*. Grampa leaned over with a lit match, but she pulled it back and smiled. "I'd just like to hold it, if that's alright."

Grampa blew out the match and dropped it on the table. "It's your cigar, sweetheart. You can eat it if you feel so inclined."

"You know those things are going to kill you, Grampa."

Grampa answered my downer without even looking at me. "Natalie, do you know what happens to rabbis at death?" She shook her head. "If a rabbi has enough time to meditate and calm himself, he can entrust his *katra*, a Hebrew word which means. . ." He blew out a puff of smoke and squinted at it. "I suppose in English, 'soul-memory.' Something like that. He entrusts his *katra* to a suitable carrier. In my case," he pointed his cigar my way, "our man Solomon. The bearer must undertake a journey to Israel, to deposit the *katra* in the Hall of Minds at the top of Mt. Zion."

Natalie played along. "Then what happens?"

Grampa shrugged, closing his eyes and looking

up. "I'm afraid I'm sworn to secrecy. Suffice it to say, I can't *really* die. Not once I'm livin' it up on Mt. Zion." He looked at me and sucked in a fog bank of cigar smoke to illustrate his point. He then turned towards Natalie and blew three perfect, doughnut-sized smoke rings at her. She thrust her hand through one like a ghostly bracelet, enamored.

I sighed. "Grampa, a *katra* isn't a Jewish word, it's Vulcan. You're just plagiarizing *Star Trek II: The Wrath of Khan*, when Spock puts his soul in McCoy with a mind meld." When had the buzzard even *seen* *Star Trek*?

"Leonard Nimoy is Jewish," Grampa explained.

"So is William Shatner," offered Natalie.

Grampa winked at her. "Exactly!"

She winked back, opening her mouth and nodding in an over-the-top gesture. They laughed.

"Finished with your waffle?" I asked. She nodded. I took my plate and hers to the kitchen and inserted them in the appropriate dishwasher. "Would you like to see the rest of the house? We have a fireplace."

I walked to the living room and struggled to light the damn thing. Natalie didn't follow. Where was she? She had come over to see *me*, not my impish ancestor. After a few minutes she walked in carrying our wine glasses and giggling. "Your grandfather is hilarious," she said, squatting in front of the defunct fire. "Need some help?"

"No," I said dumbly, striking my twelfth match. She snickered and watched the kindling light for a moment before extinguishing into a thin worm of smoke. I lit another match, swore, lit the matchbox on fire and dropped it in. It ignited in a blaze of odious zinc.

"Want to learn an old Indian trick?" she asked. I nodded. She leaned forward and connected her thumbs and forefingers to make a tiny square, which she blew through. It concentrated the air and made the embers beneath the matchbox burst into radiant flame. She smiled with satisfaction at the fire and stood up, bracing a hand on my thigh as she rose.

I sat down next to her on the couch and knocked back a mouthful of wine. Hints of laugh lines radiated out from the corners of her eyes. Most women I know hate laugh lines and do everything in their power to conceal them, but they looked marvelous on Natalie. Tiny crinkles which made her seem kind and amused without looking old. I wanted to lean over and nuzzle them.

"What's the story with your grandfather?" She raised her eyebrows over the rim of her glass.

I sighed. "During prohibition Grampa declared himself a rabbi in order to overtly bootleg wine."

She swallowed and shook her head. "No, I mean, what's the story with *you* and your grandpa?"

"What?"

"There's a lot of tension there. Did he molest you or something?" She smiled innocently.

"No, nothing like that. It's. . ." I bit my lip in thought. "Do you know what my father's name is?" She shook her head. "Judas Heinrich." I leaned forward. "*Judas* Heinrich."

Natalie whistled. "Really?"

I nodded. "Technically Grampa named him Judas Maccabees. Who was, in fact, a Jewish freedom fighter and folk hero. Has something to do with Hanukkah, I think."

"But," Natalie said, completing my train of thought, "no one in this part of the country is going to wait around long enough to hear that explanation. They're just going to hear 'Judas' and think 'bastard.'"

"Exactly. And that's my beef with Grampa. When people first meet him they think he's eccentric and jovial. But he doesn't mind letting his scams boil over the edges and scald the people around him. He was a lousy father and he's still a charlatan. I don't think it's funny to make a living as a pretend religious official, and I don't think doing it for half a century legitimizes it, either."

"Is he a good grandfather?" she asked. I narrowed my eyes. "Sorry," she said, "that's overstepping it. I'll drop the subject."

"It's okay. Would you like any more wine?"

She scrutinized her empty glass, then handed it to me. "Just half, please."

I nodded and walked to the kitchen. Grampa sat on the kitchen counter, drinking pinot straight out of the bottle. He looked like an over-sized Amish leprechaun. "Can I borrow that for a minute?" I asked.

He thrust it at me and burped. "Sitting on a couch, huh?"

"I thought a quiet evening would be nice." He snorted. I used my shirt to wipe his saliva off the mouth of the bottle. "It was either that or Former's, and she's already been there."

"Why don't you take her to a drive-in? That always did the trick for me."

"Thanks, but it's not actually 1953 anymore. Drive-ins are a thing of the past."

"Really? That's a shame." He hopped down to the floor and began rummaging for cereal in a nearby cupboard. "Well I can tell you that a raucous evening of sitting still at your grandfather's house isn't going to enamor her to you. Do you play the guitar or anything?"

"Viola," I offered. "Two years in middle school." He rolled his eyes.

"I'm going to head to my bedroom," he said. "And lock the door and turn off my hearing aids. Not because I expect you'll keep me awake, what with your invigorating chat about playing *viola*, but just to give you both some privacy."

"Okay, see you tomorrow."

"Shalom and goodnight." He poured milk into his cereal bowl and disappeared down the hall.

I slathered a smile back onto my face and returned to the living room clutching the bottle. Natalie had located the book I'd left on the coffee table, *I Only See Them When my Camera is Broken*. A collection of interviews about the paranormal, from America's premier radio host conspiracy theorist, Charles Gander.

She tittered and thumbed another page. She looked so contented and wholesome in the light of the fireplace. I was overcome with desire, but not lust. Not impulses to mount her, but to slip an arm around her waist or feel her head against my shoulder. I found myself wanting to hold her feet, to make sure they weren't cold. Love, I guess? I'm still not sure.

She noticed me and laughed and began to read aloud. "'Although most Bigfoot sightings are reported in the Pacific Northwest, numerous encounters have been reported in Oklahoma, northern Texas, and the Ozarks. In Oklahoma, the creature is variously referred to as the Noxie Monster, the Green Hills Monster, the Boggy Depot Monster, and the Fouke Monster. Sightings occur throughout the wooded eastern half of the state, but abound in the heavily forested and mountainous southeastern quadrant.'" She set the book down and held a hand over her face, trying to stifle a giggle.

"We're talking about my profession here," I said with mock sincerity, sitting beside her. I filled up her wine glass.

She continued the oratory. "'The first Bigfoot sightings can be traced to indigenous Native Americans who speak of 'the Windigo' in their folklore. A tall, hairy creature endowed with frightening supernatural powers.'" She took a sip and looked at me. "Good stuff, Saul. Isn't this in National Geographic?"

"Bah!" I snatched the book back. "You're just jealous because my taste in literature extends beyond boring dead people, like yours."

"They're not all dead," she countered, standing up. "And anyway I want to take a walk. Finish your wine." She kicked back the pinot noir, smacked her lips together and set the glass down on the floor. I took an incremental sip of my nearly-full glass, then gulped it as Natalie hoisted it from the bottom, giggling as I choked on the onrush of wine.

We exited the house into the crisp night air. Around us, the windmills twirled and creaked like colossal wooden scarecrows. She slipped a hand around my waist and hooked her thumb through a belt loop. I slid an arm around her accordingly, feeling the hint of her right buttocks arch as she moved.

"Are we walking to anywhere in particular?" I asked.

"We're strolling," she said. "But we can stroll wherever you like."

"Okay." I ushered us down a row of sleeping vines towards the winery barn.

Natalie glanced at me. "Can I ask you something?"

"Sure."

She burst out laughing. "Bigfoot?"

I blushed. "Well, I figure I have the rest of my life to enjoy office work, and—"

"*Bigfoot?*"

"Okay," I said, looking up at the stars. "I actually find it interesting. I *like* the possibility that there is something bizarre out there, something unexplained. It's romantic."

"Bigfoot," she said slowly, drawing out the playful derision, "is *romantic*. Saul, this explains so, so much about you!"

I unlocked the door to the barn and slipped inside, shutting the door behind her. I flipped the lights on and walked around, showing Natalie the various cauldrons and drums and bottling machines.

"Would you like to try corking?" I asked.

She snorted. "Maybe some other time."

I rolled my eyes, then filled up a bottle of pinot noir and used the vacuum extractor to pull the air out before yanking down on a lever to set the cork.

"Neat," she said. She tried one of her own and held the bottle up to observe her handiwork. "This really makes me want to visit a ketchup factory."

"You can have that bottle," I said. "Bring it home to the family wine rack and use it as a conversation piece."

"Thank you." She looked at me in a manner so direct and focused I felt momentarily unnerved. "I think I'll try it now, actually." She located a corkscrew and dug in. "I like that you all use real corks, by the way. When I was in Gevaudan a lot of the vineyards were starting to switch over to screw-on caps. They say it's just as good, and the wine is less likely to get fungi and stuff."

I fetched a couple of taster glasses and set them down on a stool next to her. "Grampa thought about that, but he decided the *thwip* noise is too integral to the wine experience. I agree with him." She poured the pinot into the glasses and we clinked them together. "Keep in mind that *normally* we would let this age for a few months, maybe a year. The tannins are going to be pretty sharp."

"Delicious," she offered, grinning at me with wine-stained teeth.

I took a sip and smiled back. "Actually, I kind of like the tannic kick. Gives it more of a bite."

She laughed at me. "Your teeth are already purple. You look like a moron."

I shrugged. "And you think your teeth are pearly white?"

She glanced down at my teeth again and, for just a moment, bit her lip. I leaned in towards her and closed my eyes.

"Saul."

I sighed. "Yes?"

"I like you as a friend."

"You were thinking about kissing me just then."

"Maybe. But I'm heading back to Vanderbilt next semester, and you're leaving town soon. Aren't you?"

I nodded. I felt an aching, powerful urge to hold her.

"Then let's not complicate things."

I leaned forward again and kissed her. A soft, tentative kiss. She looked down at my hands. "Saul, you're trembling!" I was. My hands shook. I get jittery whenever I have to speak in front of a group of people and, far worse, whenever I'm excited around a girl.

"Take it as a compliment," I mumbled.

She took a step towards me and grasped my hand. She squeezed it. "I'm going back to Vanderbilt next semester." I nodded. "And you're... I don't know what your next step is."

"Me neither."

"So we shouldn't get attached."

I shrugged. "Too late for me, Natalie."

She smiled sweetly and tilted her head. "I'm going to head home, okay? I'm glad I got to see you before you took off."

I nodded. "Me too. Thanks for coming over."

She put her palms against my shoulders and leaned in, planting a light, polite kiss on my lips.

Then she leaned forward *again*. This time kissing me longer. I put my arms around her and we melted into the embrace.

And then we were off—making out with reckless abandon, groping and kissing and eventually knocking stools over. After we knocked down our second stool she pulled her gray turtleneck off and smiled at me. I grinned back, and happily trembled, as she leaned her hips into mine and began to unbutton my shirt. I had suspected, and often ruminated on, what she might look like topless. She still wore a bra, but it was enough. She had an insanely well-proportioned figure, and I could feel my brain shutting down, one evolutionary rung at a time, as my body responded to her.

"We're not going to have sex," she said.

"Okay," I said, kissing her neck.

"Not now, anyway."

"That's fine."

I ran my hand through her hair and Natalie reached down to brush the front of my pants. "Why *hello*," she said, reaching down again to cup me. I had an erection you could bend horse shoes around. She held onto it and made a line of kisses from my neck to my sternum.

"Saul, do you want to . . ."

"YES."

"Uh, do you have any . . ."

I fumbled in my back pocket for my wallet. I found a battered condom which appeared to have been purchased sometime during the Reagan administration, then put through a rock tumbler. "Oh thank God," she said, unbuckling my belt.

She dropped to the floor and pulled me on top. We tore each other's clothes off like they were on fire, and jammed the condom on with the same frantic desperation of a jetliner passenger strapping an oxygen mask on during a plummet. It set the pace of our lovemaking, which Natalie conducted with the harried intensity of someone whose life depends on achieving orgasm.

We engaged in erotic feats so spectacular that, I

can only assume, we scrambled radio waves throughout the tristate area and tampered with seismological readout charts. Sex hormones bellowed forth from our passion like a furnace, arousing everything downwind of us all the way to Mexico, including certain types of rocks. When our hydraulic thrusting peaked we mutually erupted in orgasms so magnificent, so cosmically monumental, that legions of angels blushed and quietly avoided eye contact with one another.

I collapsed next to Natalie in a heap. For a few moments of postcoital bliss my pleasure-swamped neurons rewired and I thought I could taste color. She laid her head on my shoulder and draped her leg over me.

"Do you want to sleep here tonight?" I asked.

"I can't. My parents…"

"Oh, right," I laughed. "I forgot that your town is located in the 1950's."

She rolled her eyes. "It's so stupid."

Natalie stood up and looked for her clothes. In our haste to disrobe it looked like a laundry machine had exploded inside of the barn. I put my hands behind my head and appreciatively stared at her as she picked her way through discarded underwear.

She put her hands on her hips. "Are you going to walk me to my truck?" she asked.

"Yes, of course."

"Then *you* should be getting dressed, too." She threw my shirt at me.

We exited the winery after dressing and I held her hand as we walked in silence through the vineyard. When we reached her truck I kissed her deeply and slipped my hands into her back jean pockets.

"Saul?"

"Mmm?"

"Don't give up on Bigfoot just yet, okay?"

"Okay," I said. She opened her door, then leaned forward to rummage through her glove compartment. "What are you looking for?"

She climbed back out and held a silver square triumphantly in her hand. "Another condom!" She smiled, then opened the door to the back seat of her truck and pulled me in.

Chapter 12

"Little Pig, Little Pig, let me in!"

—The Big Bad Wolf, *Story of the Three Little Pigs*

So Natalie convinced me through feminine wiles to dawdle in Nambersaw a bit longer. The whole "werewolf" thing still concerned me, but I had to weigh that bloody spectre carefully against several other factors. Here is a formula which outlines the various issues I was considering:

STAYING IN NAMBERSAW

SEX:	**Guaranteed!**
DEATH:	**Maybe**
WEREWOLVES:	**. . . Probably?**
HUMIDITY:	**Irrelevant**

I'll also point out that we had only had sex twice[3], but both forays into lovemaking were so spectacular that the threat of werewolves was not enough to scare me off. I also blithely assumed that werewolves, like snakes or flood damage, are potentially dangerous but nothing some well-planned safety preparation can't handle.

I elected to remain in Nambersaw, but to abandon my Bigfoot hunt and focus instead on

---

[3] Once in the barn and once in her car! Remember?

interviewing locals—the risk of getting devoured in the woods just didn't justify the ape search anymore. So the day after Natalie and I hooked up I strode into the woods to retrieve my gear and research log.

My tent had been ransacked by racoons, as I expected, but they left the rest of my campsite reasonably unmolested. The racoons managed to unwrap all my granola bars, but the little tins of wieners and spam had clearly vexed them. I found my research notes and slipped them into my backpack along with whatever food and utensils I could locate.

Just as I pulled out a trash sack to clean up any evidence of my campsite (this is basic outdoor etiquette) I heard something nearby. Werewolves were still on my mind, but it was broad daylight, and I was flush with sex hormones, so not overly worried. I took a few steps and then smiled at the sight of three feral hog piglets scrounging for acorns.

Southeast Oklahoma and northern Texas are not going to be for want of wild boars anytime soon. As I understand it, they're descended from domesticated pigs brought over by Europeans, who escaped into the wild and turned nasty before crossbreeding with Russian boars brought over for hunting. The hybrids are fierce, omnivorous creatures averaging between 110 to 130 pounds. They're large and mean, and have four tusks which get up to five inches in length.

I squatted down to observe the piglets. Solid black, with patches of hair on their backs. Kind of cute, but not cute enough I would feel bad about eating one. Their mother turned up but did not see me. Or perhaps she did, but did not consider me a threat. Boars can be nasty and dangerous, but they're not skittish, like deer.

Then poppa boar turned up. Who *did* see me. The hairs on his back raised like bristle. He let loose a blood-curdling squeel and charged me. I clamored up an oak tree and heard the crash of tusks against bark beneath me.

You might think it's cowardly to be treed by what is effectively an overgrown undomesticated pig, but you've probably never seen a wild boar, either. Consult your local hunting lodge about how dangerous a horked off feral boar is, and you'll understand why my instincts propelled me up the limbs so fast. Wild boars are to pigs what linebackers are to cricketers.

The boar circled the tree below me, grunting and squealing and letting me know it was going to perform a cheap appendectomy for me with its tusk just as soon as I descended. I broke off a dead limb and chucked it at the boar, but that failed to pacify it.

The piglets finished foraging and laid down next to their warm sow mother in a thicket of bushy cedars. The boar sat its ass down, still facing the tree, glowering up at me. "Fine," I said. "I think I can outlast the attention span of angry bacon." I climbed up further to find a comfy resting spot. I took off my backpack and hung it from a branch, stretching out on a thick limb with my back against the trunk. I sighed, watching my breath crystallize in the air. How cold would it get before my escape, I wondered?

I put my hands behind my head and considered what new avenues I might pursue in my new suburban-oriented Bigfoot research. Then, almost within seconds, I started thinking about Natalie naked.

Hours passed. I ate lunch. More hours passed. I thought about Natalie some more. I made dinner. All up in the tree. Every few minutes I would glance down to determine if the angry boar had come up with anything better to do. Nope. They'd probably be knocking my skeleton out of the tree with a pole right now if it had not been for the ominous howl which rolled through the landscape at dusk. Beneath me, the boar stirred. It stood up and cautiously sniffed the air. After a few suspicious glances around the woods it slowly sat back down.

Then the wolves descended on him—three of them.

They didn't waste any time, either. They attacked the boar in lightning-quick unison, making a sound not unlike what would happen if you tossed a pig inside a laundry machine. The boar flew into a rage, barreling at a wolf with its head lowered, making the sound of a squeaky radiator belt about to catch fire. As it charged, the other two wolves lunged for its neck, drawing blood. The boar snapped its head to the right and gored one of the wolves in the shoulder.

The boar and the pack continued jousting, but it quickly became evident that the feral hog was on the losing team. It got in some terrific jabs, even impaled one of the wolves in the side, but each strike came at the cost of more rips and bites. After a few minutes the boar tired from loss of blood, and the wolves came in for the kill. They tore at its jugular until it dropped, then ripped the boar apart until the squealing finally stopped.

I watched the grizzly scene in morbid

fascination. And as quietly as I possibly could. Because if my drunken conversation with Uncle Amos about the existence of werewolves was as accurate as I thought it was, the animals beneath me were the same ones who had devoured those rednecks two nights earlier.

Then I noticed something out of the corner of my eye: a flash of pink. I swiveled my head, and gasped. A toddler stood not thirty feet from the carnage. A naked two or three-year-old boy, dreamily hobbling over dead leaves and twigs. Inspecting rocks, his hand, what bark tasted like.

I could barely process the sight. It was *cold* out. I had been stuck in the stupid oak tree for hours and my ass and fingers felt numb. All of a sudden the fantastical supposition about werewolves fell away, leaving only the reality of a baby in the cold, dark woods. And reality said: the toddler was in serious danger of losing his fledgling genitalia to the elements before the genitalia ever had a chance to get him into trouble. More importantly, there was a nearby *pack of wolves* gorging themselves on a brutally slaughtered boar. The little tyke wouldn't stand a chance.

I quickly made a new formula to consider these factors:

SHOULD I RESCUE THE TODDLER?

BABY: Probably dies if I leave it alone
WOLVES: . . . Possibly werewolves
HUMIDITY: Still irrelevant

As you can see from the above, it seemed unfair

to risk the baby's life on the possibility that my drunk uncle and I had successfully proven the existence of werewolves. So I resolved to rescue the kid.

I pulled myself up to a standing position and walked out as far as I could on the limb, supporting myself with other branches. I jumped down, rolling to spare my ankles and to mitigate the *thud*. For the moment, the wolves on the other side of the oak tree could not see me, nor the toddler. I quickly maneuvered towards the kid, tip-toeing through the dead leaves and twigs, each step sounding like a cannon blast in my ears. I bent down to scoop up the toddler and pressed on, all in one fluid motion.

Once a little further away I slipped into a trot. My instinct was to climb up a tree again, but it was getting dark out and the child was naked. It wouldn't take long before he submitted to hypothermia. I pulled off my jacket and wrapped him up in it.

Then the kid screamed. Not an "I'm hungry" scream, but a wail which could signal to all mothers in the tri-state area that some weirdo was kidnapping him and the cops should aim high. "Shh! Shh!" I urged. "It's going to be fine. Please be quiet! We need to be quiet, okay?" This only alarmed the toddler further. He thrashed around, screaming and kicking his legs. "Stop!" I hissed. "The wolves will hear you!"

And they did. Behind me, an angry roar echoed through the trees. I broke into a sprint. Careening around scrub oaks and jumping over logs. A chorus of howls joined in, the three wolves in pursuit, maybe more. I frantically searched for a tree to clamor up. All cedars. Un-climbable.

"Shit!" I yelled. "Shit, shit, shit." I continued

running, nearly tripping over a root. The wolves were going to eat me. They were going to tear me and the baby limb from limb. I glanced down at the kid and nearly dropped him.

The toddler had sprouted hair. Dark tufts of fur on his cheekbones and chin. Still flailing and screaming, undergoing a psychotic Rogaine nightmare.

"Well, *fuck*," I said, realizing that I had been right about the werewolves in the first place. Life sure is funny sometimes.

The wolves closed in. Howling, barking, charging through the woods. I surged forward, blindly searching for something, anything.

And then I spotted it: a shed! An old stone edifice with a slumping wooden roof. "Thank God!" I exclaimed, hustling towards it.

I dashed to the door and flung it open, falsely anticipating a lock. I chucked the hysterical Ewok baby inside and slammed the door shut behind me, huffing and about to pass out. A dusty yellow bulb flickered to life as I flipped an old switch. I locked the door and slid the dead bolt, checking to make sure the windows were too high up for wolves to leap through. They were.

I took a deep breath and dropped to the floor. "Okay," I said, gasping. "Okay." I noticed a doggy door jaggedly carved into the larger wooden door I had just shut. Panicking, I leaped up again and searched for something to prop against it. The inside of the shed had an old chair, a hat rack, and boxes of clothes. I spotted a rusty storage trunk in the corner and lugged it to the door, jamming it against the dog flap. It thumped forward as a body tried to come through.

I shoved the trunk back again and braced it as another wolf body slammed itself against the door. And another. Ten minutes of shuddering volleys, one after the other, several nearly pushing through. Lupine battering rams.

After what seemed like hours, they stopped. I dropped to the floor. I needed to find another heavy object to prop against the trunk. Finding none, I flew open a closet door to discover a rusting water tank. I gave it a jerk and dragged it across the floor. I kicked the trunk out of the way and barricaded the dog flap with the huge metal contraption. I could barely move the thing myself, and reasoned that the wolves would crack their skulls apart before budging it too far.

Finally secure, I turned my attention to the hairy toddler. He was gone. Or, rather, transformed. In the corner of the shed a puppy huddled in the corner, whimpering. It looked at me. Then it pooped.

*

One of my most vivid memories from childhood is hearing coyotes from our backyard in Hoople. In the summers my brother Jacob and I used to camp behind the house in a beat-up tent and eat candy bars and tell ghost stories. When we finally ran out of things to talk about we would fall silent and listen to the baleful howls of coyotes in the distance. Way out there, beyond the field of twitching moonlit wheat stalks, baying at a swollen, pumpkin-colored moon. Lonely songs hearkening back to the dawn of creation.

To stubby youngsters raised in a household of secularized faux Jews, the coyote wails were the holiest noise we had ever heard. A primeval chorus connecting us to the land, reminding us that our house and gadgets were just shiny toys and the *real* world was older and bigger than we would ever comprehend.

I can recall those howls making me tingle next to my brother in the tent. But they did not make me shiver the way the wolves did that night in the shed.

I don't know how many surrounded me. At least six, I think. Tireless, horrifying lurkers who never ceased prodding and clawing at the dog flap, just in case I let my guard down. Scratching at the walls, digging next to the shed, snarling and growling, vigilant for an unseen entry point. Every few minutes their din would fall silent and I would begin to nod off, then one would let loose a terrible howl and the pack would join in and I would shudder and break out in a cold sweat.

I sat in the shed's single wooden chair with my back to the wall. The toddler seemed much happier and comfortable as a puppy. And that *was* the only explanation. The only way in or out of the shed was the barricaded door. The little tot had sprouted fur and sharp canine teeth and now looked a great deal like a fuzzy miniature husky. Werewolf hypothesis confirmed.

It occurred to me that the wolves outside probably only half wanted to kill me. Half of their motivation was probably retrieving the pup. But, I reasoned, if I opened the dog flap for even a moment, a wolf would burst in and kill me. So it looked like me and the pup would have to keep each other company until I figured out an escape plan, away from the wolves.

No, not wolves. *Monsters.*

I fidgeted it in my chair, biting my nails down till they bled. I didn't think wolves could find a way in, but *werewolves*? Canine aberrations endowed with the cunning of man? How long would it take them to burrow beneath the floor boards, or crash through the roof?

I stood up from the chair and looked around. Specifically, for a weapon, although more than anything I just wanted to distract myself from the horrifying clamor seeping in through the windows. Except for a few derelict items like the water tank and chair, the shed had nothing but boxes of clothes. Old, out-of-date apparel, the sort of low-budget items you find at thrift stores. And my copy of *The Prince of Tides*. I found it underneath a pair of dusty jeans. Definitely my copy, too—Natalie's name sprawled across the top edge in neatly printed block letters.

I returned to the chair and opened the book, but the puppy yipped. I looked up. It ran in a circle wagging its tail, darting behind piles of clothes. "Hey there," I said. I walked over and tried to pet him. Overcome with delight, the puppy scurried throughout the room in wobbly loops, weaving in between boxes of clothes and darting through my legs. "Well, I'm glad at least *you're* not frightened."

He located an old ragged teddy and gripped it between his teeth, violently shaking his head. "What've you got there?" I asked. His tail zipped back and forth, nearly throwing the pup off balance. He lifted his head, proudly displaying the teddy bear. When I made a motion toward it, the pup playfully tumbled away from me. I chased him around the shed for a few minutes, feigning a desperate desire to snatch his teddy bear, grateful for the momentary distraction.

When that got old we engaged in a tug-of-war. After a few minutes I snatched the bear and we played fetch until the puppy lost interest and dropped it. He waddled over to the corner to pee, then came back and tentatively sniffed my ankle. I reached down and gave him a pat. His tail started wagging again, so I dropped to a squat and scratched him behind the ears.

"Good boy," I said, wiggling his head back and forth. He flipped on his back and yipped again, flopping around on the floor. "Who's a good boy? You are! Good boy." I rubbed his tummy and tickled him, prompting a flurry of happy kicks.

Then I poked him in the wrong place, or something, because he nipped at me. A quick, instinctive bite on my index finger. "Ow! Dammit!" I said, jerking up. I frowned at the tiny puncture marks and sucked on the blood oozing out.

Outside, the wolf glee club roared louder and louder.

I looked down at the puppy.

I looked at the fresh bite mark on my finger.

"Oh," I said. "Nuts."

*

Five forty-five in the morning found me tired and nerve-wracked. I began to understand how shell shock can psychiatrically cripple someone—one sleepless night of howling nearly unraveled me. The wolves quieted around four o'clock in the morning, but they did not leave. Every few minutes one would sniff and scratch at the dog door, just in case I had chosen that moment to remove the water tank and make a break for it.

The puppy lay curled up in the corner, snoring. I sat in the chair, keeping an eye on the water cooler and the door. Several hours earlier multiple wolves had teamed up in a concerted attempt to force the heavy machinery out of the way. They nearly succeeded, but I used all my strength to push on the tank from the opposite direction, keeping them at bay.

Now I could hardly keep my eyes open. If the wolves didn't intensify their siege soon, spiking my adrenaline levels, I would pass out. I glanced at the bite mark on my hand. The skin around it looked red. Infected.

Someone knocked on the door. I bolted upright.

"Hello?" a man asked. "Hello, is anyone in there?"

"Yes, I am!" I said, standing up. Help had come!

"Thank God! Let me in!"

I started to pull the water tank away, then stopped. "Who is it?"

"What the hell do you care?" the man demanded. "There are *wolves* out here! They'll be back any moment!"

"How do I know you're not one of them?"

"*What?!* Are you crazy? Open the door! Please! Can't you hear them?"

"Come to the window," I said. "Let me take a look at you."

"Just open the door!"

"I will, I will!" I cried, balling my fists. "But I need to see you first!"

"They're coming! Please, *please!*"

I put my head in my hands. Was I going crazy? Had I conjured up the whole werewolf idea in a fit of sleep depredation? I couldn't let the man outside be ripped to shreds because I honestly thought *monsters* were trying to devour me. I ran a hand through my hair. "Just come to the window!"

To my right, a figure slid into view. I couldn't make him out through the dirty glass. I put my face up to the window and blocked the light out with my hands.

Arno Phenris. He pulled his lips back in an eerie grin.

He cackled. "Hello, Saul. *Almost* got you."

I backed away, tripping over a pile of clothes. I grabbed the chair with my left hand and prepared to break a leg off if Phenris came in through the window. He didn't. He might be able to break the glass and crawl through, but the window was high and would necessitate a lot of squeezing. During which time I could bash his head in with a chair leg while he scraped his belly across glass shards.

"You're a smart boy," he said. "Now open the door and I won't kill you."

"Fat chance," I said.

"I'll come in through the window."

I ripped off a leg from the chair and brandished it. "Why don't you give that a shot?"

He nodded, thinking, then laughed. "Saul? Can we hold on for a moment?" I glared at him. What trick was he up to now? "Do you know what this

153

reminds me of?" He took a step back and cupped his hands around his mouth. "Little pig, little pig, let me in!" With the proper cadence for the children's' story.

"FUCK YOU!" I returned. "How's that for a hilarious fairy tale? EAT SHIT AND DIE!"

Arno's smile drained away. A cold, haunted look took its place. "I'm not in a toying mood, kid. Do you have any idea how terrible it feels to go from wolf to man? It's the worst fucking hangover you can imagine. All those bones and sinews stretching out, snapping into funny positions. Organs twisting and rearranging. Don't screw with me right now, Saul. I'm going to ask you once. Nicely. What have you done to my son?"

"What?" I asked. "You mean the werewolf pup?"

He glared at me. "Is Channing in there or not?"

I put my hands on my hips. "Yeah, he's here. He's sleeping."

"Let me see him."

I walked over to the corner and scooped the puppy up. I returned to the window and held him up to the light, nearly dropping him as he wriggled around in my hands. "We're friends," I said. "He's fine." He swung his head around and licked my nose.

"Friends?" Arno growled. "You kidnapped him! You kidnapped him and you killed his brother!"

"I didn't kidnap him. Look, I didn't *know* you were werewolves! Not until last night. I saw a naked toddler wandering near a pack of wolves, and I tried to save him. I had no idea he was your son. Also," I added, feeling a sudden self-righteous kick, "You stole my book!" I picked up *The Prince of Tides* and shook it at him.

Phenris nodded, scrutinizing my face for signs of dishonesty. "Okay," he said. "I believe you about Channing. Let's talk about making an exchange. Your life for his."

"Look," I said, exhausted, "I'm stuck in this shed, and you're out there. You've got the cards and I know that. I'm not going to hurt the puppy, so you can quit worrying about it. But neither of us are leaving here until you fetch a police officer to personally escort me away."

He snorted. "A police officer? Where would I find a police officer?"

"Go to Lycan."

"Lycan!" he laughed. "No, they're forbidden to come into our territory. They know that. And I'm not about to invite someone from Nambersaw onto my land."

"Well, then I guess we're stuck with the status quo."

"I'll starve you out."

"No," I said, picking up the puppy. Channing. "Because you're not going to let your son starve. I'll push the water tank back a little and you can slide some food in through the doggy door, if you'd like."

Arno lowered his voice, affected a raspy softness. "Saul, listen. We're going to talk man to man, okay? Channing's mother is frantic. She thinks you're going to kill him. Here's my deal: I'm not going to kill you. Today. You *thought* you were protecting a kid, and I respect that. So I'll let you walk out this time. Just this once. But you have to open the door and return Channing to me."

"Why should I trust you?" I asked. "I open the

door, you burst in and kill me."

"It's very cold outside," said Phenris. He took a step back and gestured to his exposed genitals. "You know I'm naked, right? Can you slip some clothes through the door?" I shook my head. "Okay, you want to know why you should listen to me?" I nodded. "Be very quiet for a few moments."

"Why should—"

He held a finger to his lips. His eyes glinted maddeningly. "Listen."

At first I didn't hear anything. Then. . . something. Scratching. From below. I set Channing down and pressed my ears to the floorboards. They were burrowing. Digging a tunnel beneath the shed, slowly undermining my defenses. I stood up and faced Phenris in the window. "Do you hear it?" he asked. I nodded. "You have an hour, maybe two. Then we come up through the floor."

I leaned against the wall and rubbed my face. I was so horribly, unbelievably tired. I wanted to sleep, to cry, to be anywhere but there. "You won't kill me if I open the door?" I asked.

"I won't kill you *today*."

I sighed. "Alright. Fine." I dragged the water tank out of the way and unbolted the door. I took a step back and inhaled deeply, not sure if a pack of wolves might break through to kill me. "It's open."

Phenris kicked it open and loomed in the frame. Naked. A wicked halo from the rising sun surrounded his steaming figure. He looked at the chair leg and snorted. "Drop that. I find it disrespectful. You're safe for the moment, I give you my word." I lowered it to the floor. Slowly. At this point, if he wanted me dead, a chair leg wasn't going to do a lot against a pack of wolves.

"Good," he said. "Channing!" The puppy careened towards Phenris, barely able to contain his enthusiasm. Channing squirted urine across the floor. Arno picked up the puppy and nuzzled him, clutching the wriggling mass of fuzz against his hairy, muscular chest. "A few minutes ago you said we were 'werewolves.' Can you define that?" He stroked the puppy.

I cocked my head. What was he getting at? "A werewolf is a man with the ability to transform into a wolf."

He nodded, digesting the information. "That definition doesn't strike you as a little. . . anthrocentric?"

"I don't follow," I said. "I'm really very tired."

"All I'm getting at," he said, voice of a lawyer, "is that I think you're approaching the phenomenon backwards. What would you call a *wolf* that turns into a *man?*"

I walked to the door and nudged him out of the way. He smelled unlike any person I'd ever met. Feral. "I'm not sure."

He turned to face me. "Think about that," he said. He pointed to his right. "I imagine you'll want to head to Lycan. It's that way."

"Thanks. Thanks a lot." I started trotting in the indicated direction.

"Saul?" he called, when I had already jogged a distance. I looked over my shoulder. "I'm not a werewolf, Saul. Don't ever call me that again."

"Frankly," I yelled back, "I hope I never have an opportunity to do so."

He smiled at me. Even from the distance, and in

157

the dark, I could see two huge incisors extending over his lips. "Not by the hairs of your chinny-chin-chin?"

He cocked his head back and chortled.

The wolves howled along.

Chapter 13

"Wolves are not our brothers; they are not our subordinates, either. They are another nation, caught up just like us in the complex web of time and life."

—Henry Beston

I caught my second wind as the sun rose. I felt exhilaration at the prospects of not being mauled, and still a little nervous that I might be. Thus, I managed to keep a steady cantor despite the terrible drain of energy and stress undergone in the shed siege. I jogged down the trail and through the woods, popping out into the same dairy farm I parked next to the first time I entered Lycan. At the bottom of the slope two men stood loading jugs of milk into a large van. I headed their direction, intentionally rustling through the dead grass so as to not scare them.

"Good morning," I said.

"Morning," they chimed. On the left stood a dairy farmer, clad in overalls, boots and a cowboy hat. On his right stood some kind of delivery man. Slacks, a button-up shirt and a serviceman cap, all mountain peak white. Topped with a black bow-tie. They didn't seem particularly alarmed to have me run into them at five thirty in the morning. "Where are you headed to?" the delivery man asked.

"Do you know the Rougarous?"

He nodded. "Sure, I just saw Maurice the other day. Care for a lift?"

"Yeah," I said, "that's really nice of you."

"No problem. Hop in."

His vehicle was an oversized van with a giant plaster milk bottle bolted to the roof. "Wargson's Dairy" was painted in neat block letters across the side. A healthy version of an ice cream truck.

I buckled my seatbelt and shivered. I wiped the excess snot from my nose and rubbed my frigid hands together. The driver hopped in and turned the van on, letting the engine warm up. "Ralph," he said, extending a hand my way.

"Saul," I offered.

"Whoo!" he whistled. "Your hands are *cold*. Let's turn on the heater for you, huh?" He rotated a knob, ushering in a welcome gust of hot air.

"Oh, wonderful, thank you."

"Don't mention it. Do you like Bing Crosby?" he asked, sliding a cassette into the tape deck.

"I don't know. Up until just now I thought he was a cartoon character."

"Nope." The truck sputtered away from the dairy.

"So you're a delivery man?" I asked.

"Milkman," he corrected.

"A milkman?" I asked. "I didn't realize they still existed."

He smiled happily and shifted gears. "There are a few holdouts left. A lot of the families in town prefer fresh unpasteurized milk to the store bought stuff. So they're willing to pay a little to find jugs of local dairy milk on their door each morning." He laughed. "But we're too few to form an effective union, that's for sure."

I glanced at my watch. "It's five forty a.m. and

160

you've already loaded up your van with milk. Isn't it exhausting to wake up so early?"

He shrugged "You saw Rudy Wargson back there? Here in about an hour he's going to sit down to a nice lunch. Besides," he gestured beyond me and through the window to the rising sun. "I never get tired of that. And I like mornings. They're fresh and peaceful. Excuse me," he said, parking the truck.

He hopped out and opened the back. I sat there, eyes bloodshot, energy drained from a full rotation of adrenaline bursts.

Ralph hustled up a frosty sidewalk to the front door of a one bedroom house. An otherwise neatly manicured lawn, suffocated by bird baths, rocks with inspirational phrases on them and a lawn gnome population crisis. I expected him to set the milk down and jolt back, but he patiently stood on the welcome mat, tilting the jugs to glance at his watch.

As if on cue, the front door opened and a tiny blue-haired woman emerged from behind the glass storm door. I couldn't hear what they said, but their body language conveyed casual, meaningless chatter. "Have a good week so far?" "Oh, yes thanks. Sure was a pretty day yesterday, wasn't it?" That sort of thing.

Ralph said something which made the blue-haired woman laugh. She took the milk jugs from him and disappeared inside, returning seconds later with a cup of coffee. He took it and thanked her, then pointed toward the van and said something else. She nodded and waved to me, then retreated into her house. Ralph twisted his torso my direction, winked and gave a thumbs-up. Moments later she returned with a second cup of coffee, which Ralph handed to me as he climbed into the truck.

The little woman waved at us and I mouthed "thank you" before the truck rolled away. "Mrs. Damarchus. What a sweetheart. Every morning she makes me a cup of coffee. How nice is that?"

"Very," I said. It did strike me as a powerful way to raise job satisfaction.

"Did you know she was homecoming queen once?" He laughed. "You wouldn't guess, though, not from your view. But if you talk to her up close, you can tell. She just has this look, you know? Deep down, she knows she's pretty." I nodded. "Would you like sugar or cream? You'll find some in the glove compartment."

I opened it and decided on two packets of brown granulated sugar, as opposed to the tiny envelopes of white creamer. "Thank you. You're quite prepared for hitchhikers, aren't you?"

"Sure, ha! Excuse me." He parked the truck again, this time on a residential street in the town itself. He made his rounds for four different homes before popping back into the truck, cheeks red from the early morning cold.

"Brr!" He pointed to a derelict Buick parked in one of the driveways. A nice model, but peeling paint and deflated tires. "See that car?" I nodded. "That's Mr. Pinetum's. He hasn't moved the thing in years. People keep offering to buy it off him (it's vintage or something), but he refuses to sell it because he wants folks to think there's someone home when he goes out for groceries."

He laughed. A wholesome, white-toothed laugh which I imagine had never contained even a grain of malice in the history of its punch lines. "But see how the tires are deflated? That car's not fooling anybody."

"Would you like me to run the milk to the door?" I offered. "Then you wouldn't have to keep running back to the truck to pull it forward."

"What?" he asked. The idea had obviously not occurred to him. "Nah, it's cold out there. You sit tight."

"No, really. Think of it as cab fare."

He laughed. Despite the fact Ralph was in his thirties, he had three tiny pimples on his forehead. As if he was so overwhelmingly Caucasian that his whiteness had started clogging his pores. "Well, okay then. But I'll have to tell you which houses, alright? About half the folks don't use our service. Here we are." He parked on the next street and indicated which homes needed milk. I hopped out of the truck and shivered, immediately regretting my offer. I flung open the back doors and grabbed some milk jugs, then delivered them, sprinting across lawns to lessen the time in the frost.

I got back in and shoved my hands against the warm air vent. "Okay, I've got the next few," he said. He pulled onto Main Street and waved at a passing truck. "That's Rambaud. Mr. Pinetum's son. He's the editor for *The Lycan Bugle.* I eat lunch with him every Thursday."

Ralph gave me an informal tour of Lycan as we made deliveries throughout the next three blocks. He pointed out the home of Michelle Verdung, the high school sweetheart he pined over from ages seventeen to eighteen. Now he was the godfather of her children, and had coffee with her husband Robert every Monday.

He dropped milk off in front of Mr. Rollet's two story cottage, the elderly middle school principle who retired three years ago before an abundance of free time drove him to the brink of insanity. The school subsequently invited him back as "Principle Emeritus," which included an office but no salary or specific duties. He showed up to work every day.

Ralph pointed out Rachel Poligny, who sold her family bar-b-que to start a record shop, which bombed two years later. But, he said, she took it with stride. She tried, she failed, she moved on. "What more can anyone do?" he asked. We drove past the home of Peter and Cynthia Stubbe, who operated the town's mortuary and moonlighted as clowns for children's birthday parties. I couldn't tell if that was endearing or the creepiest thing I'd ever heard. Probably the latter.

"Do you know everyone in town?" I asked.

"Everyone who's not lactose intolerant. Excuse me." He delivered six more jugs of milk and returned to the truck. "So where are you from, Saul?"

"Hoople, originally, then everywhere."

"Really?" A look of recognition played across his face. "Oh, you're the boy who ran over Arno Phenris's dog, aren't you? Accidentally," he added, to sound less accusatory.

I looked out the window. If I squinted, the homes dotting the street looked like gingerbread houses. "No," I said, "I'm the guy who ran over Arno Phenris's son. But you all know that, don't you?"

I looked to Ralph for signs of shock or confusion, but he said nothing. A tight-lipped, pristine, *Father Knows Best* poker face. He flipped on the turn signal. "Bray Road." He parked the truck in

164

front of the Rougarou's. "Would you take their milk for me?"

"Sure," I said.

"Two jugs." He stuck his hand out and shook mine, but withheld a smile. "Nice meeting you, Saul. Good luck to you."

"You too. Thanks for the ride." He nodded politely before leaning over to pull the door shut. I fetched the jugs from the back and trudged up the driveway to the house, watching the lactose mobile chug away. I checked my watch when I got to the front door. Six thirty. Should I ring? I hesitated, then knocked. Situations involving werewolves trump usual etiquette about waking folks up.

After the second knock the door opened. Dr. Rougarou stared down at me, perplexed, wearing a thick flannel bathrobe and giant bear-foot slippers. "Saul?" he asked. I nodded. He poked his head outside and shivered. "Ah! So cold! Come in, come in!" He put a hand on my shoulder and pulled me inside.

"Sure is a surprise to find you here this morning," he said. "Normally the milk arrives *without* a suitor for my daughter. Let's fix you up with some orange juice or something." I followed him into the kitchen and handed him the milk jugs. He stared at my face and grimaced. "Saul, you look awful. You didn't walk here from Nambersaw or anything, did you?"

"Well, yes, but with a long break in the middle."

He nodded. "Well, that's good exercise, I guess. Everything okay?" He turned around and walked toward the refrigerator.

"No, sir. I just spent twelve hours locked in a

shed, defending myself from werewolves."

He dropped one of the milk jugs, which clattered to the floor and spewed all over the tiles. Maurice stared down at it, dumbfounded. "Don't cry over spilled milk," he muttered, turning to deposit the surviving jug into the refrigerator. I watched him clean up the milky glass shards in awkward silence. "I need to get dressed and go to work. When I come home tonight we'll talk about what happened. Can you stay for dinner?"

"No," I said. "I don't think you understand— I got *attacked by werewolves.* I don't want to wait for dinner, I don't want to hang around anywhere. I want an explanation, which I think you have, and then I want to go back to Nambersaw and lock every door to my house and sleep for twelve hours."

"Okay," Maurice said softly. He stared at me intensely, making his mind up about whether or not to confirm what I already knew. "Let me wake up Cally and Natalie. We all ought to be here for this."

We assembled around the kitchen table a few minutes later. Natalie was blurry-eyed, and looked younger and softer without any makeup. Cally looked both tired and frightened. Maurice set cups of coffee in front of us all. He sat down gently across from me at the head of the table. The early morning sun filled the room with a soft, blue light. I'm not often up early enough to see the light of dawn, but it definitely has a different shade than sunset, which leans orange.

"Saul," Maurice said, taking a deep breath. "Arno Phenris is a werewolf."

The three of them looked at me expectantly. "No shit?" I asked. Cally's eyebrow raised at the curse word. "Werewolf," I repeated folding my arms. "I got attacked by *werewolves*." I let the sentence hang there, like an accusation.

The Rougarous all seemed very uncomfortable. I wondered if they had ever given Natalie a sex talk, or if that had been indefinitely tabled. "Right, of course. And you also know that Arno is my cousin?" Maaurice asked. I nodded. He folded his hands on the table, and peered into his coffee. "It's time we let you in on the secret, then. One that we do not reveal to people outside of Lycan. Ever. I'm going to ask that you *absolutely* refuse to mention anything about it to anyone else."

"Okay."

"Good. Arno isn't the only werewolf. As you've no doubt realized, there is an entire pack of them. They live in the woods outside of Lycan, but their range extends well into the Quachita National Forest. Mostly they keep to themselves. Sometimes they come into town for medical treatment or supplies, at which point they're awkward . . . but civil."

"Awkward *but civil?*" I asked. I leaned forward and tapped the table as I spoke. "We *are* talking about the man who attacked me in a diner? And the werewolves that killed some meth heads before blowing their house up?"

"I see your point," Maurice said. "Forgive me. *Until recently* our town kept an uneasy truce with the werewolves."

"Where did they come from?"

"I'm not sure," he said. "But they've been here awhile. Maybe as long as the town itself. Lycan started out as a French fur trading post in Wichita territory. There's evidence that the original Wichitas

167

who lived here had a strain of lycanthropy, and fled into the woods as more and more settlers came. We do know that a little after the Louisiana Purchase another wave of Frenchmen moved in from the bayous around New Orleans. I think they probably brought the werewolves with them."

"And you. . . allowed that?"

Maurice shrugged. "I don't know how the town responded at first. The werewolves probably integrated into the community before we ever realized what they were. And by then it was too late to do anything."

"Too late?" I asked. "What about pitchforks and silver bullets and stuff?"

Dr. Rougarou folded his arms. "Who would we have used them on? Our brother-in-laws? Our next-of-kin? Arno is my cousin. Half the pack is somebody's second or third cousin. Despite what you've seen in the movies, it doesn't strike us as ethical to chase down and kill things we don't understand."

"Besides," added Cally, "you're assuming they're evil. The werewolves don't skulk around town at night preying on children. They live in the forest. They hunt wild animals. We live in the town. We go to the grocery store. Until recently we never had a conflict. There's an old rule that they can't enter Lycan unless on two feet, and we stay out of their territory. Lately they've ignored it, but it's worked remarkably well for the last hundred years."

"I saw Arno Phenris kill three men," I said. "They got attacked by a pack of wolves, then Phenris blew their house up with a Molotov cocktail. How is that peaceful co-existence?"

Maurice stroked his mustache for a few moments before responding. "That was regrettable. But you have to consider things from their perspective. We keep saying 'werewolves,' but we haven't qualified the term. Some time ago, I don't know when exactly, the werewolves living in town moved out to the forest full-time. They effectively quit human society. Sometimes they revert back to human form, but day-to-day they're *wolves*. From their perspective, our laws don't apply to them. Those men you saw get killed chased after Arno's daughter with rifles, and I'm told earlier in the week fired shots off at a wolf. The pack saw them as a territorial threat."

I wanted to continue arguing with the man, but in my sleep-deprived state couldn't dredge up the necessary rhetoric. I actually kind of liked Stewart, but they *were* running a meth lab and marijuana plantation, and probably intended to kill me for finding it. They weren't exactly model citizens. "You've been talking like werewolfism—"

"Lycanthropy," Mrs. Rougarou corrected.

"What?" I asked.

"Lycanthropy. It's the medical term for the condition of becoming a werewolf. If there were a medical term for becoming a werewolf."

"Okay," I said slowly, turning back to Maurice. "You've been discussing lyncanthropy like it's inherited. How did Arno become one?" I dropped my hands beneath the table. "Did they bite him?"

Maurice shook his head. "Every few years someone from town decides to join them. Usually loners, people who just can't seem to find their place in modern society. Arno always wanted to be a forest ranger, and I guess one day he decided he'd rather be a part of the forest."

"How?" I asked. "Spells? Magical ointment?"

He laughed. "No, Saul. It's a disease."

I plopped my hand on the counter and pointed to my finger. "How is it spread?"

Maurice craned over to look at my hand. "They bit you?" I nodded. "It's spread by blood, not saliva." He patted my hand. "You should be fine."

"Arno married a woman with lycanthropy," Cally interjected, "contracting it through intercourse. Others in the past have taken blood infusions. Anything else you want to know?"

"Yes," I said. "Why do they want to kill me? Is this all because of the. . . the wolf I ran over?"

Maurice and Cally exchanged glances. "Arno's son, Lowell," said Maurice.

"You had no way of knowing," Cally said, resting her hand on mind. "None of us blame you for that."

"But it *is* why," Maurice continued, "there have been so many domestic disputes recently. Arno wants blood vengeance. We won't let that happen. Neither will the town. As a result, the werewolves have been. . . trying to intimidate us. Extending the bounds of their territory."

"How safe am I?"

Maurice stared at me for several moments. "Arno is a hothead. And he's not used to thinking like a man. Remember that almost all of his waking hours are spent as a wolf. If I were you, I'd get out of the county. He won't drive a car after you. I'll go into the woods tonight—"

"No!" blurted out Cally. "Maurice, you can't—"

He held a hand up. "Cally, I'll be fine. Arno is my cousin, werewolf or not." He turned to face me. "I'll go into the forest tonight and speak to Arno. Try to reason with him. He's still grieving the loss of his son, albeit poorly. He'll ultimately reach the conclusion that it was a mistake, an accident, and no one is at fault."

"Until we're sure it's safe, I don't think you should come to Lycan anymore," said Cally. "Except during daylight hours. But always be gone by nightfall."

I looked at Natalie. "It won't be a problem," she said. "I'll just go to Nambersaw. We'll hit up Former's."

I nodded. "Fine."

"Would you like breakfast, Saul?" asked Cally.

"No, thank you, Mrs. Rougarou. I think I'll just head home."

"I'll drive you," Natalie said, scooting her chair back. I walked with Natalie to the door with her parents in tow.

They both hugged me as I stepped out and onto the porch. Maurice put a hand on my shoulder. "I know this is weird and frightening Saul, but it'll all get sorted out. I promise."

It didn't, but it was nice of him to say so.

*

Natalie glanced away from the road towards me. It was the most exhausted day of my life, and somehow I could not go to sleep. As if I were too *tired* to fall asleep.

"Are you angry?" she asked.

171

"Yes," I said. It hadn't occurred to me at the kitchen table, but now that she asked, I *was* pissed off. "I just spent two and a half months living in danger of werewolves. And you never stopped me, never warned me. I kind of understand wanting to conceal your relatives from the public, but you all screwed up regarding *me*."

"I'm sorry." She bit her lip. "We didn't think you were in any danger, okay? Normally the wolves stay away from people. They don't want to be found out. And you were living in a tree or on the vineyard."

"Arno Phenris *attacked* me the first time I came to Lycan!"

"As a man, yes. But we didn't think he'd come after you as a wolf."

"I think you should kill him," I said. "He's threatened to kill me, and he killed three people without a trial. Correction, he's now *told* me he's going to kill me. He's dangerous, and you should put him down. Maybe he has rabies," I added.

Natalie turned onto the highway. "Have you ever heard the story of the werewolf of St. Almo?"

"No."

"It's one of the stories they tell us growing up. Some time ago in Italy the town of St. Almo had a werewolf. A very nice young man, actually. The townsfolk realized what he was during his childhood, but they couldn't bring themselves to kill him. And he only turned into a werewolf on Christmas anyway."

"What?" I asked. "Why Christmas? That doesn't make any sense."

She looked at me quizzically. "Christmas is the

holiday associated with werewolves."

"No it's not," I said. "That's Halloween. You never hear about yuletide wolves."

"I follow your logic," she agreed. "Monsters on Halloween, Jesus on Christmas. I'm just telling you that, in folklore, werewolves are always associated with Christmas."

"But that's—"

"Just go with it," she said. "It's incidental. It's only a part of the story."

"Okay. So the Italian turned into a werewolf annually on Christmas."

"Right. But the rest of the year he was fine, a model citizen. He got a job, got married and everything. It's just that once a year the town had to accommodate his condition. On Christmas Eve, everyone would go home and lock up. His wife would kiss him goodbye and he'd leave the house, and neither she nor anyone else would open their doors until the next day. Usually somebody would wind up missing a sheep, but he'd pay them back, and everybody was happy."

"Arno doesn't sound like that to me," I said. "I think he'd be an asshole even if he were human 365 days a year. Even on Christmas, which remains a ludicrous day to associate with wolfmen."

"The moral of the story is that good people can be afflicted by things beyond their control. And good townsfolk, us, take care of our own, even if there's an element of danger."

We drove the rest of the way to Nashoba Vineyards in silence. She parked her truck and smiled at me. "I bought new underwear," she said.

"I am still angry."

She shrugged. "Okay. Well, let me know when you quit being angry, because I'll probably be horny then. We can try 'corking' again."

"Okay," I said slowly, exiting the truck. I sensed, rightly, that I had somehow conceded the argument without meaning to. She sped off, waving back to me as she drove.

Chapter 14

"He who makes a beast of himself gets rid of the pain of being a man."

—Samuel Johnson

I had a lovely autumn, despite constantly looking over my shoulder for fang-toothed psychopaths. My research grant to discover Bigfoot expired and I sent in an embarrassing synopsis of my field research without even a shred of hard evidence supporting the existence of an undiscovered ape. A month later, to my astonishment, I received a warm letter from the Anthropology Department at Wiley College congratulating my fine work. I realized that academia could not care less about tangible results or measurable output, and so promptly applied for a follow-up grant on the relationship between bluegrass music and ghost sightings.

With my grant concluded I no longer qualified as an anthropologist, but merely as a college graduate looking for work. Nambersaw felt a little too sleepy and boring[4] for a twenty-three-year-old such as myself, but I took up Grampa on his offer to make me Assistant Vintner until I could figure out what the hell to do with my life. And I didn't mind sticking around the vineyard for a few months if it meant proximity to Natalie.

---

[4] Except for the werewolves.

I have been in love on a handful of occasions, but never had the good fortune to realize it at the time. In Natalie's case I don't think it was the usual fear of commitment and emotional intimacy which shielded me from otherwise happy realizations of limerence. Rather, I think I was too busy falling in love with her to be self-aware of the plunge until after it happened. And, being twenty-three, it was easy for the sexual fireworks to distract me from the deeper tug at work.

We spoke on the phone for at least an hour every night, sometimes talking well past two in the morning. It's probably a good thing we had some geographical distance between us to compel these phone chats, because whenever we met up in person we could barely keep our clothes on long enough for decent small talk. After she finished up at the ranch Natalie would drive to the vineyard and use our shower, which we would have sex in, before heading to the bedroom for more sex, sometimes followed by dinner. (Then sex.)

At one point, we shook the bed in the guest room apart, which is an accomplishment I am still proud of—I would like that particular detail of my sex life included in my eulogy someday.

You might think: "It was probably an old bed, with loose joints, and the headboard would have eventually dislodged anyway."

No. You are absolutely wrong. We shook that bed to death with a sexual prowess known only to the most virile of superheroes, or possibly Olympic athletes snorting steroids and Viagra. I am confident that if the technology existed to harness orgasms as an alternative source of fuel, our thunderous lovemaking could have lit up the entire Midwest like a Christmas tree.

I digress. In between turning each other into happy fountains of body fluids, I became familiar with the day-to-day operations of the vineyard. Grampa and I tended the complexities of the winery while the Mexicans finished pruning and tidying up the vines for winter. If there was nothing else to do, I would erect pole-mounted speakers throughout the rows of grapevines and wire them to the new CD player at the house. In retrospect, I don't think Grampa's scheme of blasting Baroque music at grape clusters did much to improve their flavor, but it did lend an ambience to an already comely chunk of the county.

Most days Grampa would explain how something in the fermenting process worked, then delegate it to me before lighting up a cigar and reading a week-old newspaper in a recliner he'd dragged into the wine barn. On two occasions he fell asleep like this and the newspaper caught fire, but the old man miraculously survived both combustible moments without any injuries.

By Friday of my third week as Assistant Vintner he quit showing up. I had a handle on things, he said. Come get him if there was a problem. Soon there was.

We had lowered the wine vat temperatures to just above freezing in late October. This is so tartrite crystals stick to the sides, pulling some of the harmless but ugly clouds of sediment out of the wine before we drain it. On this day, the malbec vat approached room temperature, two days ahead of schedule. I tried to figure out the problem with the cooling but could not locate the point of issue. So I went looking for Grampa.

If Grampa could not be found in his house or at the winery, it meant he was hanging out at the bunkhouse with the Mexicans. He paid them well below what we might consider the "legal" federal minimum wage, but then, they were all illegally living in America, too. In this regard the laborers found a surprising champion in Grampa, despite his occasional (and colorful) use of racial epithets. Grampa firmly believed in the sanctity of private property, or at least of *his* private property, and was perhaps the only voter in the county opposed to immigration controls. As he saw it, he should be allowed to employ whoever he wanted on his own property, and Uncle Sam had nothing to do with it. So he never bothered informing Uncle Sam of the several farm hands he provided room, board, and wages to. Or, presumably, his actual taxable income.

The scant linguistic bridge connecting Grampa with the day laborers no doubt helped things. Whenever one or the other couldn't get their point across, everyone would smile awkwardly to convey, "we're all friends here." Had Grampa been unfettered by language difficulties he certainly would have gotten around to pissing them off. As it was, he liberally handed out cigars, and for reasons which still mystify me, commanded a warm loyalty from the farm hands.

I walked across the property to the edge of the vineyard and knocked on the bunkhouse door. Somebody yelled "Entre!"

The bunkhouse was at least spacious. And, except for the slanted ceiling and rafters, bore little memory of its earlier life as a horse stable. The building had been scrubbed clean, with no trace of hay or manure. Each individual horse stall had a dresser and a bunk bed, so that every pair of Mexicans had a shared cubicle and some semblance of privacy. A card table sat in the middle of the open area, surrounded by Grampa and five half-naked Mexicans playing strip poker. Probably with one of Grampa's marked decks, although I doubted they knew it.

"I'll stay," Grampa said, oblivious to my entry. Pedro dealt a card to the Mexican next to him, then nervously glanced around the table. After a few moments, everyone threw down their hands. "Pay up, amigos!" he exclaimed. He flicked his cigar ash into an old coffee can and laughed triumphantly. His employees grumbled, removing belt buckles and watches and passing them around the table.

"Grampa?" I asked.

He looked up. "Saul, glad you're here. Pull up a seat."

"No thanks, I'm here on business."

"Dandy," he said, finishing his stogie and dropping it into the coffee can. "I had another brilliant idea."

"Before you interrupt me, I—"

"Boxed wine!" He announced, holding a hand up majestically. A couple of Mexicans applauded half-heartedly.

"Sure, but—"

"I was against boxed wine for years, you know. But then I came up with a clever play-on-words, and thought, what the hell?"

"The Grapes of Wrath vat is—"

179

"'Wine^3: *Drink Outside the Box.*' Get it? It's a math pun, too." He cackled. "We'll load it up with sugar and market it to college students." He held out his index and middle fingers in a V. "Puro, por favor." Miguel withdrew a cigar from his shirt pocket and placed it between the old man's knobby digits.

I sighed. "That's great. Really. But I thought I should tell you that the Grapes of Wrath vat is at room temperature."

Grampa set the cigar between his lips and leaned forward so Miguel could light it. He took a couple of puffs and leaned back in his chair. "I checked it this morning and it was fine."

"Well, it's not cold now."

He nodded, puffing. "Should be alright at this point in the process. What day is it?"

"November 20th."

He sucked on his cigar thoughtfully and shrugged. "That's alright. We'll just make a note to get the cooling mechanism fixed. We can correct for whatever crystals are left using the bentonite here in a couple of days. I'll teach you how."

"Okay then," I said. Grampa took a long, ponderous puff on his cigar and studied his cards. "One more thing," I said, shifting awkwardly. He cocked an eyebrow.

"The wolves."

"Los lobos!" Miguel said. The Mexicans all crossed themselves, muttering.

"They're fine," Grampa said, waving a hand at me. "I got 'em covered."

"Right," I said slowly. I had brought the topic up with him on several occasions, but he always changed the subject. "Grampa, I think there's something very peculiar about these wolves."

His eyes flickered at me momentarily. "Yup," he agreed. "But rabbis are sacrosanct. It's a well-known fact that wolves can't kill a man of the cloth. Hit me," he said, pointing to the dealer.

"Well," I said, "we're still in trouble then. Because, as you'll recall, you're not a holy man—you made our family religion up yourself."

The old man shrugged. His pale blue eyes sized me up, and for a moment, almost seemed pleading. "I didn't make up Balaam."

"Who's that?"

"He's in the Torah," Grampa said. "Bible, too." He cocked his eyebrows, as if inclusion in *both* books signified a tremendous about of gravitas.

"Never heard of him."

"He was a non-Jew," Grampa said. "And a 'wicked man,' to boot. But this heathen, who worshipped false gods and served the enemies of the Israelites, he still possessed divine gifts. He could curse people, bless people."

". . . Okay," I said.

"What I take from this," Grampa went on, "is that you don't necessarily have to be properly ordained, or even know the right stuff let alone believe it, to find yourself vested with powers in some cosmic drama." He arched his eyebrows. "Understand?"

"Not really," I said. I assumed Grampa was merely justifying his charlatan antics—nothing more.

"You'll figure it out eventually," he said, returning to the poker game. "Any requests for Thanksgiving dinner? And notice I said 'dinner.' I figure hell, once or twice a year I can afford to skip breakfast."

"A change of pace sounds nice, but I'm spending Thanksgiving with Natalie."

Grampa folded his arms. "You're *skipping* Thanksgiving?"

"The Rougarous invited me over for dinner at their house, Grampa."

He maneuvered the stogie from one corner of his mouth to the other using only his lips. "You can't skip *Thanksgiving!* Everybody's coming! Amos, Betsy. . . even the Mexicans!" He gestured to the half-naked men shivering around him. "It's going to be a damned *feast.*"

I shrugged. "Grampa, I'm sorry, but I'm really excited about Natalie. This is a big step."

Miguel leaned forward. "They break the bed," he said gravely. He turned to the other poker players. *"Rompieron la cama."*

Several Mexicans nodded enthusiastically.[5] Pedro gave me a thumbs up.

"You broke the—" Grampa's eyes widened, then he kicked his head back and roared with laughter. "Alright," he said, wiping his eyes. "Who am I to stand in the way of *that.*" I turned bright red with embarrassment, and he guffawed, choking on cigar smoke. "Fine, enjoy your Thanksgiving."

He took a deep drag on his cigar and locked his piercing eyes into mine. "But I want you to plan to be here for Hannukah this year, Saul. Because I think it

---

[5] I may have bragged to a few people about the time Natalie and I broke the bed.

will answer a lot of the questions you have about *Los Lobos.* And if you prove your worth, I'll teach you the rites. So that one day *you* can preside over the Festival of Lights."

He turned back to the poker table and dealt out playing cards. "Someone has to," he muttered.

*

Natalie invited me not only to Thanksgiving, but to a play the night before it and a tacit invitation to sleep over. When she called me the previous week I had thought it was some sort of local theater venue, but it turned out to be an elementary school production her cousin Rebbecca was in. *Thanksgiving Comes to Lycan,* written by Jack L. Rollet, Principle Emeritus.

If you take out all the kids forgetting their lines, not speaking loud enough, hitting each other in frustration, missing their cues, and hiding behind curtains from stage fright, I guess it was an okay production. Spectacular by Podunk twelve-year-old standards, I guess. Anyway, I liked the story.

It was the French and Indian version of Thanksgiving, which struck me as far less ominous than the Pilgrim and Indian version I grew up with. As a member of the Choctaw tribe, I always listened to teachers explain Thanksgiving with nervous suspicion. I recognized at an early age that if the Indians had done the sensible thing and let the pale-faced religious fanatics starve to death, Mississippi might still be populated by my kinsmen instead of the gun-toting rednecks who drove them out.

At the beginning of the play the French explorer

183

Bernard de La Harpe establishes Lycan as a canoe hub for fur traders. It soon grows into a French merchant outpost, but the Gaulic beaver hunters make it clear to the surrounding Wichita tribe that they're only interested in skinning cute animals, and see no real benefit to a land which otherwise strikes them as unfit for human habitation. They do insist that the Wichitas swear an oath to the French king, but that's about it. The Wichitas think, "Wow, these guys are way nicer than the English. Let's slap a Fleur-de-lis on a tepee and see if maybe we can get some guns out of this."

Then winter strikes. (I could tell because the little kids wearing fake beards all acted as though they'd spontaneously contracted Parkinson's disease, and a kid backstage lobbed a bucketful of cotton balls at them which landed on the floor in a clump.) The French run out of provisions and have sour luck hunting for deer, and are close to resorting to cannibalism. Then a friendly band of Wichitas decides to bail them out and brings over a bunch of corn and ham, and everybody has a great big Thanksgiving feast.

Except that, unlike the English version, the French fur traders decide they're tired of being bachelors, so they all marry young Wichita girls. Thus, Lycan lurches into existence as a Franco-Indian community. I was so happy that the Indians had the good sense to marry their daughters off to the guys with guns that I gave a standing ovation at the end.

Afterwards I went up to find Mr. Rollet and shook his hand. I recognized him as the befuddled, basset hound-faced man I had met months earlier at the diner, moments before Arno Phenris grabbed my throat.

Mr. Rollet graciously accepted my compliment, but in a distracted way. I figured he was trying to remember who I was. "Thanks, thanks," he said. "The real talent is our youngsters. How are your parents doing?"

"They're fine, thanks, much happier since the divorce." He nodded but continued to look perplexed. "I'm not from here, if that's what you're wondering. We've only met once before, when I asked you if you'd seen Bigfoot. I'm Natalie Rougarou's boyfriend."

"*Oh*," he said. "Good. Well. I was afraid I forgot another name. I'm down to about ten, now. Yes, Natalie's a wonderful girl. I used to be her principle, you know."

"So I've heard."

"I'm in the Rotary Club with her father. Tell him hello for me."

"I will."

I showered ill-deserved compliments on Natalie's cousin, still dressed like a Wichita princess, before we finally left. We drove back to the Rougarou house, but took an extra twenty minutes to get there and probably endangered a lot of lives due to the interesting things we did to distract each other on the way.

When we got to the Rougarou's home Natalie's mom hugged me at the front door, and Maurice stuck his head out from the kitchen to yell hello. "How was the play?" he asked.

"Pretty good," said Natalie.

"Best version of *Thanksgiving Comes to Lycan* I've ever seen," I said.

"Glad to hear it. Saul, would you come here and give me a hand with the cider?"

I brushed the small of Natalie's back with my finger tips and walked to the kitchen. Maurice thrust a hot mug of apple cider into my hand and broke out in a toothy Teddy Roosevelt grin. "Shh," he said, pulling a bottle of rum out from the back of the spice rack. He poured us both a healthy glug and winked at me before stashing it away.

Over the next hour it became obvious to everyone that Maurice could not hold his liquor. His cheesy grin only disappeared long enough to put food in his mouth before plastering across his face again. He persisted in smirking and winking at me, as if we were co-conspirators in an epic prank. Mrs. Rougarou seemed more amused than irritated, feigning ignorance of her husband's mischief. Natalie seemed annoyed at first, but then she excused herself to the kitchen and came back with a mug of cider, and seemed more content thereafter.

I helped Natalie rinse the dishes after dinner. "My dad is such a dork," she said.

"I think he's funny."

"Maybe."

He stepped into the kitchen and poured himself another mug of cider. "Can we celebrate something?" he asked. "I feel like we should be celebrating something." Natalie fished the rum bottle out of the liquor cabinet and handed it to him. "What's this?" he said, feigning comical astonishment.

"Dad," Natalie chided, "everyone knows you're drinking. Let loose, you only get drunk once per pope."

He bent down and kissed her on top of the head. "And now you're old enough to join in with me. So that's what we're celebrating. Saul? Want to join in?"

"Of course."

"Nobody tell the wife."

"She knows," Natalie intoned boredly.

Maurice dismissed the idea, handing us both a mug of spiked apple juice. "*The Jerk* is going to come on after the next commercial. You a Steve Martin fan, Saul?"

"Indeed I am!"

Maurice beamed. He slapped a hand on his knee. "Well! Let's go to the den already!"

For the next two hours we watched *The Jerk*, with the nearby fireplace blazing and popping. During commercial breaks Mrs. Rougarou would excuse herself to the kitchen, returning with tall glasses of water she made us all drink. Then the movie would resume and she would slide onto the couch next to her husband, tittering away at Steve Martin as Maurice giggled.

Natalie and I sat together on the love seat under an afghan. I could feel her body tense with embarrassment each time her parents snorted. I liked it, though. Most of my friends' parents still desperately cling to the idea that they are cool, that they are abreast of trends in fashion and are only temporarily using minivans. The Rougarous suffered from no such delusion, if they ever had. They were dorky and oblivious, and it made them tremendously endearing.

By the time the credits started rolling both Mrs. Rougarou and Natalie had sacked out. Maurice delicately extricated himself from his wife's slumping figure and turned the television off. "I'm not quite ready to sleep yet," he said quietly. "How does one more cider sound? Just a standard one," he clarified. "I've got to get up tomorrow."

I nodded, trying not to dislodge Natalie from my shoulder. He returned shortly with more cider and padded over to a record player I had previously thought was ornamental. He thumbed through a couple of vinyls before setting a Billie Holiday record down on the rotating disk. He returned to the couch and looped his arm around Mrs. Rougarou. Neither of us said anything, for fear of disturbing our respective women. We just sat in the glow of the fire, sipping cider and listening to *Lady in Satin.*

I don't know why I started crying. I'm sure there's a simple psychological explanation for the embarrassing faux pas. I have no real home town, no high school to claim as my own. My parents are divorced. My existing family was just a loose collection of lecherous weirdoes with a common surname. The cider, the crackling fireplace, the warmth of Natalie, her goofy parents. It was all just too much.

Maurice took it in stride. The easiest way to make a man feel uncomfortable is to start blubbering in front of him. I kept it quiet, but I could feel hot tears leaking out the corner of my eyes and dribbling down my cheeks. Dr. Rougarou betrayed no sign of discomfort. He remained fixated on the fire, a look of drunk, absolute contentment shining across his face. Near the end of the record, when I finally got a grip on myself, he swiveled his head to give me a sympathetic smile and slow wink.

My chin quivered and I looked at the floor,

charging the entirety of my will power with the task of holding myself together. I felt something I had not in years.

Home.

*

The next day I woke up as Natalie quietly shut the door to the Rougarous' guest room behind her. She put a finger over her lips and stepped out of her pajamas, then slid into the bed next to me. We cuddled for a few minutes as I groggily bobbed in and out of consciousness. Then, when she grew tired of waiting, she climbed on top of me and my eyes fluttered open.

She put a finger over her lips and pantomimed a variety of over-the-top orgasm faces. I giggled, then murmured as she slid a condom over me. We proceeded, with moderate success, to make love as quietly as we could, ineffectually using a pillow to muffle her. When we finished we held each other and stared into one another's eyes from three inches away. I grinned at her like an idiot, and she grinned back.

Then the sounds of breaking glass startled us out of our idyllic postcoital daze. I pulled a pair of jeans and a shirt over my pajamas and followed a hastily-dressed Natalie down the stairs. "Everything okay?" I asked.

Mrs. Rougarou, frazzled and in a bathrobe, was crouched down in the living room picking pieces of broken glass out of the carpet with her fingers. Maurice stood next to her, frowning and holding a brick. "Someone lobbed this through the window," he said.

"What? Why?"

"I don't know." I followed him outside to the lawn. The neighborhood was trashed. Most of the brick mailboxes had been knocked over, broken at their bases. Trashcans lay in the middle of yards and driveways with their contents spewed across the grass. Someone had scraped a key along the side of Maurice's truck. Natalie's passenger side window was cracked in a huge spider web pattern.

I looked back at the house and saw the first of the graffiti. "SKINWALKERS!" was painted across the front door in dripping red paint. The neighbors' door across the street bore "FREAKS!" Looking down Bray Road I could see that each house had some other mark of vandalism sprawled across it.

Maurice appeared calm, but he clenched his jaw so tight it looked like he was smuggling ball bearings in his mandibles. The knuckles on his clenched fists were white. "Who did this?" I asked.

He jerked his head up and down, glaring at the wounded street. "Phenris and his gang," he muttered. "A bunch of teenagers, mostly. Marking their territory."

I checked on my car. The Volvo managed to survive the Kristallnacht with only a pile of trash dumped across the hood, but the lack of damage did little to cool my increasing fury. I surveyed the Rougarou house. In addition to the broken window and front door graffiti, someone had spray-painted an entire phrase across their garage door: "WHO ARE THE REAL MONSTERS?

"Those *bastards!*" I seethed. "Those miserable sons of bitches!" I could not recall ever having been so angry. I wanted to find Arno Phenris and punch him in the throat. Run a pitchfork through his guts. The thought of someone despoiling Lycan infuriated me. The act was abominable. In my few visits to Lycan I had come to think of the town as the essence of decency and small town America. The vandalism was more than just graffiti and property damage. It was an attack on innocence itself. The defacement of an original Norman Rockwell painting; rape in Lake Wobegon.

Maurice sighed. "Let's go in." He trudged through the door, deflated and exhausted. "I'll call the mayor."

Natalie and Mrs. Rougarou met us at the door. "The phone lines are dead," said Natalie. "Should we arm ourselves?"

Maurice shook his head. "No, not now anyway. They're just trying to intimidate us. If they were going to attack, they already would have. I don't think they will."

"Attack?" I said. "Why isn't the sheriff on this? This is crazy!"

Maurice lightly gripped my elbow. He turned to his wife. "Cally? Can you make us some coffee?" She nodded and disappeared into the kitchen. "Natalie, does your cell phone work?"

"Yeah." She handed it to him.

"I'm going to call Mayor Bisclavret. Make sure there's no threat. Saul, I want you to watch the front door. Natalie, you take the back. Yell if you see anything suspicious."

He returned after a few minutes with a cup of coffee in his hand. "Can I see everyone in the living room?" He handed Natalie her phone back. "I just talked to Lou Bisclavret. So far as we know, no one in town has been hurt. It seems last night was just widespread vandalism."

"Why?" I asked. "What's the purpose of wrecking the town on Thanksgiving?"

Maurice shrugged uncomfortably. "You know how small town politics are, Saul."

"Not really," I said. "But do you mean 'werewolf' politics?"

He smiled glumly. "Yes, I suppose I do." He looked down at the floor. "Arno Phenris told the town to hand you over to him. We refused."

My face grew flush and I balled my fists. *"I. Didn't. Know."*

Cally put a hand on my shoulder. "We know that, Saul. That's why the town will protect you however we can."

"I fucking hate Arno Phenris," Natalie said, walking towards the door. "I'm getting my crossbow. I'm gonna spear him in the balls."

Dr. Rougarou put a hand on her shoulder. "Maybe," he said. "Maybe tomorrow. Not today, though. Today is Thanksgiving!" Natalie and I looked at Maurice like he was trying to drum up enthusiasm for a game of shuffleboard on the *Titanic*. "That's why they did this now. To ruin the holiday, to make us feel vulnerable. Let's be angry tomorrow but grateful today. We have a lot to be thankful for, and it would be inappropriate for us to ignore our blessings because of a broken window and some spray paint."

"Yes," Cally said slowly, with a decided lack of enthusiasm. "*So much* to be thankful for." She put her best game face on and gestured vaguely to the world around her. "The foliage . . . it's beautiful."

"Hey, that's the spirit!" Maurice said. "Also, the Dallas Cowboys are shaping up pretty well this season. So there's that."

"I read that the S&P is up again," I ventured meekly.

"Oh, well *that's* good news," said Cally.

Natalie folded her arms. "I'm still going to shoot Arno in the balls with my crossbow."

Maurice gave her a stern look. "*After* lunch. But we are going to *celebrate* Thanksgiving and have a *good time*, darnit!" He bobbed his head once in an affirmative nod. "Yes," he said, apparently agreeing with himself. "Now let's all get dressed. Cally and Nat, you handle food prep. Saul and I will do what we can to clean up the mess outside and repair the window. Everything should be normal by lunch."

I threw on a vest and joined Maurice outside to clean up the junk in the yard. Even though monsters had trashed his property, Maurice seemed stoked to have a dude to hang out with at Thanksgiving. I gathered it had been awhile since male relatives had come over for the holiday, and it had only just then occurred to Maurice that, someday, Natalie would drag in a son-in-law. A prospect which clearly pleased the guy.

"We usually watch the Macy's Day Parade," he said, pulling garbage out of his mailbox, "but I think *this* year we can watch The Game." And he said it that way, capitalized. As if, between us, we commanded enough testosterone to wrench the television away from floats and marching bands.

We spent half an hour scrubbing the graffiti off his garage door while Maurice cheerfully brainstormed all manner of male bonding activities: hunting, fishing, restoring an old car. By the time we taped a cardboard flap over his broken window he had completely forgotten about the werewolf damage and had moved onto the exhilarating topic of installing a microbrewery in his basement.

We wrapped up cleaning and walked to the curb to survey the property. Maurice planted a hand on my shoulder and grinned. "Well, I can't say the cardboard matches the shutters very well, but otherwise I think it's a handsome homestead!"

"Yeah," I agreed, "it looks terrific."

He clapped his hands together. "Alright then! What's say we head into the house for some coffee?" he mock-punched me in the stomach. "Hoh!"

"Sure, that sounds great," I said. "Let me just make a quick phone call." I watched as Maurice shadow-boxed his way into the house. As soon as the door shut I called Cindy.

"Hey, mister!" she exclaimed. "Happy Thanksgiving! How's life in the woods?"

"Happy Thanksgiving!" I said. "My woodland research is over. "It's too dangerous. I'll explain later. Listen, can I ask you for a favor?"

"Always."

"I need you to make me something."

"Name it."

"Bullets. Silver ones."

Chapter 15

"Don't be startled, Sir John. You have the silver cane for protection."

—Maleva, *The Wolf Man*

I didn't see any more werewolves until December, in an unexpected but benign sighting. I had been taking a nap upstairs in Grampa's farmhouse when Amos burst in through the door and yelled, "There's a naked chick playing Frisbee in the vineyard! Lezgo!" and clamored down the stairs. I followed down after him and, sure enough, saw Naked Girl at the edge of the vineyard.

She hurled a plastic disk out over the thin sleeping hedges, prompting two enormous wolves to weave in and out of the vines before finally leaping up like dolphins at the last instant to catch it. They engaged in a tug-of-war until one secured the disk for itself. The wolf flipped its head, sending the Frisbee in a wobbly arch towards Naked Girl's general vicinity, with the losing wolf merrily following after it. Naked Girl sprinted through the rows, jumped up, and caught the Frisbee in her teeth. Then she tossed it back.

"Amos," I said, "You should know that—"

He put a meaty hand over my face. "Shhh," he said. "Just enjoy the moment, Saul." He fished a hip flask out of his jacket and took a snort, then offered it to me. For a few minutes we stood in the crisp winter

195

air, just appreciating the elegant sport of Frisbee, the beauty of the human form, and the breasts. Her mysterious origins did not trouble Amos. He is a live-in-the-moment type guy.

After a few minutes the two wolves dashed into the woods. Naked Girl faced the farmhouse and enthusiastically waved at me. I raised my hand.

"They the werewolves?" Amos asked.

"Yeah."

"Hmmm," he said. He folded his arms and watched Naked Girl retreat into the woods. "If we get mauled," he said slowly, "I'd like that blonde one to do the killin'."

"Should we go get guns?" I asked. Amos gave me a quizzical look, then pulled his jacket back to reveal a holster and a sidearm. "Of course."

Naked Girl's lupine companions *did* trouble the Mexicans. Profoundly. We could barely make them out in the dimming light. All six stood sentry in front of their converted horse stable, clutching pitchforks and rosaries, rifles slung over their backs. They waited until they were sure the wolves had retreated, then marched up to the house.

Amos offered out his hip flask, but they all declined it. "You fellas enjoy the show?"

None of them smiled. "Where is Señor Heinrich?" asked Miguel.

"We're all Señor Heinrich," I sputtered. Amos and I laughed, drunk.

"The old Heinrech," said Pedro. "Please. We find him."

"I'll get him," muttered Amos, turning to the house. "Back in a minute, amigos."

He returned a few tense, silent minutes later

with my grandfather and two mugs of mulled wine. Amos collapsed into the chair next to me and passed a mug my way.

"Yes Miguel?" asked my grandfather. He sounded serious. I wondered if he thought they were going to kill him, standing around the house with pitchforks like that. Generally it's not a good thing when armed villagers show up at the local land baron's house to chat.

"The lobos, they are much. Now, Señor, we ask for the Hanukkah"

Grampa looked beyond them, peering out over the vineyard. "It's not Hanukkah yet."

"But, Señor! Los lobos! They are—"

"Hanukkah starts in three nights, Miguel." He held up three fingers. "Tres noches." The Mexicans chattered amongst themselves. One tugged on Miguel's sleeve, relaying his thoughts in frantic Spanish. Grampa lifted his hand to silence them. "It always falls on the Solstice." He pointed up to the sky. "Hannukah *has* to fall on the Winter Solstice. Good night."

The Mexicans warily marched to the converted stable and turned every light on. I saw the shadow of one of them standing in the window with a rifle. Grampa stared up at the moon, appraising it. "You know where the term 'lunatic' comes from?" he asked. I shook my head. "Years ago it was commonly accepted that too much moonlight made people go berserk. Hence, 'lunatic.' Think about it."

"Alright, Grampa." He harrumphed and strode back into the house.

Amos took a sip of his steaming wine. "You know what?" he asked.

"What?"

"I think I got my first kiss from one of those forest nudists, like that Frisbee girl."

"Forest nudists?"

He nodded. "Yup. I was fifteen years old, and—"

"You got your first kiss at *fifteen*? Ha!"

"Simpler times, Saul. You wanna hear the story 'er not?" I shrugged. "I was out turkey hunting and I heard something, and I spun around to fire and there was a naked girl standing behind me. Peaceful and smiling, like she had no idea I'd almost flossed her teeth with buckshot."

"How romantic," I offered.

"Well it *was*," Amos stammered. "We talked for a few minutes, and she didn't mind that I was eyeball-licking every blessed curve, then she leaned forward and kissed me. I told her I was in love with her, and I was, but I never saw her again." He looked at me suspiciously. "So she was a werewolf?"

"I think so," I said.

"Hmmm. Makes you think," he said.

"I guess so."

At that moment a sedan pulled into the driveway. "Hey!" Cindy said, jumping out of her car.

"Another blonde," Amos said, putting a hand over his gun. "She a werewolf too?"

"No, no!" I said. "She's a friend!"

"Hmmph."

I crossed over the frosty lawn to give Cindy a hug. She ran to me, nearly bowling me over with the force of her full-throttle embrace.

"Hi!"

I gave her a squeeze and stepped back. "Have

any trouble finding the place?"

"None," she chirped. She dressed like she had stolen a Japanese pop star's wardrobe. A bright white-and-red polka-dot dress, tights, glittery shoes and a headband.

"Good. Let's head inside where it's warm. Did you bring the groceries?"

"Yeah, you want to carry them?" I nodded and walked to the back of her car. She handed me a brown paper bag.

"You're a doll," I said, peering over the bag. "Seriously, the old man *only eats breakfast.*"

"I think that's cute," she offered, opening the front door for me.

"It is. But after two weeks, you get to craving pasta or steak or something."

"Well, you're in luck then. I bought us smoked salmon, avocados, croissants, vinegar and cream cheese. Fish croissants aren't too breakfasty, are they?"

"No. Just delicious."

She followed me into the kitchen and started slicing the croissants open with a knife. "The rest of the groceries are just soups and things I thought you might enjoy."

"Thanks!" I said, putting them underneath grampa's arsenal of cereals. "I'll pay you back for all this."

"Don't worry about it," she said. "The food is on me. But I *do* need you to pay me back for the bullets and the silver. Silver is expensive, by the way."

"Just put it all on my tab," I said.

I heard the back door slam shut. Grampa walked in, a rare cloud of deep thought following him.

"Grampa, this is Cindy," I said, pointing towards my accomplice. "She came up to have dinner with me."

It did the trick. Grampa's womanizing instincts disengaged his moody contemplation almost instantly. "What a pleasure, what a pleasure," he rumbled, stooping to kiss her hand. He angled his head towards me, but his torso remained facing her. "How on earth do you know so many pretty girls, Solomon?"

"Dunno, Grampa."

"My dear, do you like cigars?" He put a hand to the corner of his mouth, then pulled it back, appearing to magically withdraw a stogie in the process. Sleight-of-hand.

"Sometimes," she said, "But not ones that have been in other people's mouths."

He nodded at me. "*That's* a high-class dame, Solomon. You watch yourself around this one." He retreated down the hall. A few moments later we heard a muffled *Fiddler on the Roof* rendition wheeze out of an old record player.

"Aww," she said, squeezing one of my cheeks. "You never even had a chance at being normal, did you?"

"Har har. How did the art festival in Austin go?"

She threw her hands up. "Philistines! I didn't even get 'honorable mention.' Can you believe that? I think it's because the robots look comical. You make something creative *and* funny and it's automatically disqualified from being deep. You never see comedies win Best Picture at the Oscars."

"People suck," I said, grabbing a plate of salmon

croissants. "Would you like any wine? I'm a little tired of it myself, but I think there's some merlot in the fridge. Also several dozen cases out in the wine barn."

"I'll just help myself to a glass of milk."

We ate dinner and talked for a couple of hours before Cindy checked her watch. "Hey, I need to go. I'm helping Dad feed the animals early tomorrow morning."

"Okay," I said. "I'll walk you out."

We stepped into the chilly night air and shivered. "Don't forget your bullets," she said. She opened her passenger door and took a box out of the glove compartment. "You didn't say which caliber. But I figure everyone has a .20 caliber hunting rifle."

"It's the AA battery of guns," I agreed.

"Okay, here," she said, handing the ammo to me. "These aren't solid silver. Even if I could afford that much of it, I thought about the actual process of making one and I'm pretty sure I'd blow my hand off trying." She tapped one of the bullets. "I just plated the tips. Now before I give you the rest, would you care to explain why you need ornamental ammunition? Is this some kind of bizarre birthday present for your cowgirl girlfriend? Because I can tell you, she'll appreciate bullets and jewelry a lot more than some skint combination of both."

I shook my head. "It's for a personal project. Don't worry about it."

She folded her arms. "No," she said, planting her feet. "You don't get to request a box of ammunition from me and write it off as a 'personal project.' Facts. Now."

"It's stupid. Really."

"*Of course* it's stupid," she said, "I just want to make sure it's something stupid *other* than the stupid idea I think you've come up with."

"What do you think I want them for?"

She grimaced. "Alright, I'm just throwing it out, and I know it sounds dumb, but. . . Do you plan to go blasting werewolves or something? Because that's the only reason I can think of to own a silver bullet."

My jaw dropped. "Well. . . Yeah."

She put the box of ammunition back in her glove compartment. "Okay, I'm glad I asked. How about dinner in Hugo next week?"

"Whoa," I said, "you're not going to give them to me?"

She turned around and put her hands on her hips. "So you can go gun down suspected wolfmen? No thank you, mister. You wouldn't last a minute in prison. You're too pretty, Saul."

"I won't shoot *people*," I said, "just wolves."

"Uh-huh."

"Seriously! I got attacked by some two weeks ago!" I threw my hands up in the air. "And I saw a bunch before that. And did I mention one of the werewolves plans to kill me? He told me so!"

Cindy shook her head. "No. In the last two hours you talked about your girlfriend, your girlfriend, George Lucas and whatever those tartrite crystal things are you dump in the wine. Werewolf death threats never managed to come up."

"Well, I promised someone I wouldn't elaborate," I said. I waved my hand through the air. "I can say no more."

She sighed. "That's not–" she squinted, then pushed me on the shoulder, tilting me to my left.

"Look over there. Is that. . . ?" I followed the direction of her gaze. Walking towards us through the vineyard was a pale figure. "A naked woman?" It was. Naked Girl. Strolling at a leisurely nude pace in the frigid weather.

"Hi," I said, as she approached. "How are you?"

She looked from me to Cindy. She balled her fists and glared at my friend, baring her teeth. Cindy huddled behind me. "You forgot this," Naked Girl said. She took another step towards me and put her hand out. I reached and took a book from her. *The Prince of Tides.* "Thanks. How's Channing?"

"Being a skinwalker is cold," she said. "I don't like it. I'm leaving." She spun around on her heels and strode back through the vineyard. Neither Cindy nor myself said anything until she receded into the forest.

"Yeah, she's a werewolf," I commented. "I also think she's in love with me?"

Cindy nodded, fishing the ammunition out of her glove box. She dropped it into my hands. "I don't think she's a werewolf, but that's definitely weird. *Weird*," she repeated, shaking her head. "You promise to only shoot wolves with these, right? No scruffy bystanders who wander into your paranoid delusions? No blasting guys with beards?"

I held my hand up and struck a politician's poise. "On my grandfather's Torah."

"Okay, mister." She leaned forward and kissed me on the cheek. "Don't get killed, okay?"

Chapter 16

"I hear a werewolf howling at the kitchen door
You'd better not let him in
Little old lady got mutilated late last night
Werewolves of London again"

– Warren Zevon, "Werewolves of London"

Christian parents tell their kids to bunker down early on Christmas Eve because otherwise Santa will see that they're awake and skip the house. Growing up, my father, aunt and uncle were advised to go to sleep early throughout Hanukkah because that was when golems escaped the family storm cellar and stalked the vineyard thirsty for blood. Consequently, Grampa's children were so terrified of the monster-infested storm cellar that when a tornado nearly reduced their home to toothpicks in 1962 each Heinrich child staunchly refused to seek shelter underground, electing instead to take their chances with the swirling vortex of death.

What they never realized was that Grampa's horrible parenting was in this instance based on fact. Monsters *did* stalk the vineyard on Hanukkah. Hungry beasts who might have devoured his brood had they been discovered outside after dark. I don't know why Grampa never told his heirs the truth about their grizzly childhood nightmares. I suspect that by the time they were old enough to understand the true meaning of Hanukkah–sating werewolf bloodlust—they were also old enough to hate him and disregard anything he said.

I grew up with a modified version of the Hanukkah my father experienced. In Hoople we would light a candle on the menorah and exchange presents and that was it. Grampa's Hanukkah was far more complex. It entailed hymns ranging from the "The Star Spangled Banner" to a variety of ditties lambasting Grampa's neighbor, Harry Bradford. It also involved a dreidel competition, which doubled as a drinking game and sometimes used loaded dice. Not strictly kosher.

Amos, Grampa and myself celebrated the first night of the holiday around his dining room table. Both of my relatives were weirdly preoccupied. They sang the songs and participated in the sacred drinking games, but occasionally one would look out the window, or glance over his shoulder. I got the distinct impression that the Hanukkah I was now seeing was merely a showpiece.

At eight thirty we called it a night. Amos hugged me and Grampa and headed towards the door. "Happy Hanukkah," he said solemnly. "Shalom."

Grampa flashed him the Vulcan salute. "Good night, shalom."

I went upstairs to read. I was about to begin *Der Rosafarbene Ritter* when I heard the back door creak open. From the window I could see Grampa walking towards the vineyard, his silver menorah blazing. I dashed down the stairs and quietly slipped out the back, trailing him as he marched through the vines.

The night air felt crisp and frosty. An inch of

snow lined the ground, crunching beneath my feet as I quietly stalked my ancestor. His black figure glided over the pearly terrain as a fleshy shadow, before stopping in front of the Mexican bunkhouse. Miguel stepped outside with a leashed goat. He stared at my grandfather with wide eyes, listening to the old man mumble. I could only hear bits of his incantation. ". . . Your lamb shall be without blemish, a male of the first year: ye shall take it out from the sheep, or from the goats. . ."

Miguel handed the creature over and slammed the door shut behind him. Grampa continued on through the vineyard, the goat leash in one hand and the menorah in the other, towards the wooded shadows of the Kiamichi mountains.

I pursued him in stealth, through the snow and rows of icy grape vines. Past the edge of the vineyard into the forest itself. With a blanket of snow to absorb sound, I could trail the old man from a short distance. I couldn't hear what he was saying: only the faint whisper of invocation, of endless droning.

The light of the menorah cast eerie shadows behind the trees we passed. It reflected off of the alabaster terrain and gleamed in the icicles that hung down from limbs. The light of the menorah glinted off the ice slicks, and the forest transformed into a garden of glass. Twice the menorah candles died from the breath of a bitter wind, only to sputter to life again. The sight startled me and I wondered if maybe Grampa actually *did* wield some kind of spiritual potency. But then I realized they were just trick candles he'd stuck in the menorah to thwart the angry draft.

At last he stopped in a clearing. He thrust the

menorah out in front of him to illuminate a copse of trees. He walked towards one tree in particular; a clattering, leafless asp, white as bone. Someone had carved a large Star of David into the trunk. Blocky Hebrew letters notched the bark like Norse runes. He set down the menorah and tied the goat's leash to the asp.

As he crouched over to secure the knot I saw the candlelight reflect off eyes. Three pairs of glowing green orbs stared at him from the frost-bound woods. I nearly yelled at him, but he noticed them. He stood up and snatched the menorah, brandishing it towards them like a crucifix.

A wolf, a *big* one, emerged from the rimy trees. It growled and took a step towards Grampa, but the old man didn't flinch. They stood there, eyes locked, until Grampa pointed a knobby finger at the goat. "There's your sacrifice, beasts!" he wheezed. The wolves growled, their eyes flashing in the candle light, but they drew no further.

"Eight nights!" he called out. "Eight nights. Then you stay away from the vineyard and away from the men of this land!" For a moment I saw his jaw tremble, and heard him whisper under his breath. "Until next year."

One of the wolves craned its neck to howl. More howls rose from the forest. Dozens, perhaps hundreds.

Grampa peered into the forest warily, then turned around and headed towards me. I ducked behind a tree. ". . . then he shall take one lamb for a trespass offering to be waived, to make an atonement for him. . ." he muttered, walking past me. I followed after him. Behind me, ferocious snarls mingled with terrified bleating as the wolves tore the goat to shreds.

I crept behind the old man, following him to the Mexican bunkhouse. The creaky stable was decked out. Plastic statues of Catholic saints ringed the premises like sentries. Dashboard Virgin Mary's ringed the edge of the roof like colorful Dollar Store gargoyles. Shoe polish crosses adorned every window, flickering from tea candles within. Strands of garlic dangled from doorknobs.

The door swung open. Pedro and Miguel stepped outside, both holding live chickens, both terrified and shaking. Pedro handed one to Grampa, who in turn handed him the menorah. He spoke directly at them. ". . . For the Lord will pass through to smite the Egyptians; and when he seeth the blood upon the lintel, and on the two side posts, the Lord will pass over the door, and will not suffer the destroyer to come in unto your houses to smite you. . ."

He clutched the chicken by its legs and swung, snapping its neck against the side of the former stable. He dropped the dead bird on the doorstop and received the next chicken from Miguel along with the menorah. The Mexicans bowed and returned to the bunkhouse, shutting the door behind them.

He slowly wound his way to house, still muttering. ". . . and if he be not able to bring a lamb, then he shall bring for his trespass, which he hath committed, two turtledoves, or two young pigeons. . ."

Grampa repeated the poultry rite at his own back porch, dashing the bird's brains out against the side of his Georgian edifice. He held his flickering menorah up as wind whipped around him and held a palm up to the light of his porch.

"And the blood shall be to you for a token upon the houses where ye are!" The wind rose to a howl. His raspy voice boomed over the din as the menorah flickered and extinguished. "And when I see the blood, I will pass over you, and the plague shall not be upon you to destroy you, when I smite the land of Egypt! Amen!"

He dropped the dead chicken on the doormat and walked around the house to let himself in through the front door.

The next morning the chicken was gone. All that remained were a few droplets of blood on the snow, pointed in the direction of giant paw prints.

*

On the second night of Hanukkah Grampa caved into my demands and let Amos bring Chinese food over for dinner. He even consented to let me invite Natalie over, but unfortunately she had been waylaid by the flu and couldn't make it. Which irritated me, because I was pretty sure our Hanukkah gifts to one another would have been sex.

Amos, Grampa and myself loaded our veins with boiled rice and MSG before kicking off the evening's festivities. Which I found tedious. The previous evening had been fascinating, what with its eerie faux Hebrew rites, ferocious lurkers and superstitious Mexicans. But I had only been a spectator, and a clandestine one at that. For the rest of the week Grampa intended to subject Amos and I to re-vamped saloon jingles and a twirling dreidel. And, at some point, a tutorial in the *real* Hanukkah he administered by himself at night.

Amos left after supper. Grampa poured the remainder of a bottle of Friends in Merlot Places into glasses for us while I chucked wood onto the fireplace. He handed me my glass and sank into a creaky rocking chair. "Saul, your cell phone works, right?"

"Sure," I said. "Why?"

"Can I borrow it for a minute? I'd like to call your dad. Wish him a happy Hanukkah."

I instinctively reached into my pocket, then stopped. Why did the old man want to use my cell phone? He had never showed interest in mobile technology before, in fact rather opposed it. "Why don't you use *your* phone?" I asked.

He shrugged. "It's in the kitchen, I'm already sitting down. . ."

Caller ID. That was it. Dad purchased caller ID for his house when the technology first came out, specifically to screen the calls of his erstwhile father. I had not realized they'd resumed their communication blackout, but that was surely it. "If you want to talk to Dad, you're going to have to call him on your own phone," I said. "I'm not going to trick him into answering a call from you."

Grampa rocked back and forth in his chair, swirling his wine glass. "I just want to tell him Happy Hanukkah."

"Well, send a card. Write him a letter. I don't think he'd throw out unopened mail."

He sighed. "Fine. Thanks anyway." His tone implied not defeat but disappointment. That I had somehow failed him, failed decency. I refused to accept the blandishment.

"It's not my fault Dad won't talk to you. Especially on Hanukkah, for crying out loud. Dad told me about the golem stories you made up when he was a kid. And you named him *Judas*. You should consider yourself lucky that Amos has stuck around as long as he has."

Grampa gritted his teeth. "You weren't there, Saul. If your father wants to argue with me about my childrearing panache or lack thereof, I'll listen. But you weren't around, so you should butt out."

I felt anger skitter beneath my cheeks. "You're right. I wasn't around. How about this—Dad never learned how to be a good husband because he never saw one growing up. So I've been around long enough to see his marriage fall to pieces with my mother. Or, let's consider the fact that I've never even met my Aunt Sarah, who left Oklahoma at eighteen and has never come back. So I guess she's not around anymore either, but—"

"Shut up!" he snapped. "Just, just *shut up*." He knocked back the glass of wine and poured himself another.

"Do you know what—"

"I said shut up, dammit!" He brought a fist down on the rocking chair's arm, snapping a support beam and sloshing wine on his black suit. He refilled the glass with shaking hands. "Let's take a deep breath, okay?" He rocked back and forth, back and forth, trying to regain his composure.

He noisily breathed in through his nostrils and peered at the fire. "Saul, let me tell you something. I'm old and I imagine I'll kickoff at the most within a decade. So I've been thinking about the afterlife a lot. Even a cursory look at my track record indicates I'm not in for a fun time. Hell, my police record is incriminating enough, and it barely scratches the surface." He gulped down merlot, finishing half the glass. "My point is, there's a long list with my name on it when Judgment Day comes.

"So I've thought, what kind of defense can I possibly offer God when my *katra* creeps out of Mt. Zion? Here's what I've come up with: as miserable a bastard as I am, I genuinely *wanted* to be a good person. Did you know that?" I shook my head. "Well I did. I just don't seem to have been born with the capacity to achieve it. And the other thing is this, I really do regret all the shit I've pulled. I'm genuinely sorry for all the folks I've hurt, the marriages I've broken up, the progeny I've screwed up and yes, used to beat with a belt. It's far too late to fix any of it, but I think about it every day."

I stared at him, dumbstruck. My mouth opened and closed idly. "And one more thing," he said, turning to glare at me, "you have no right being such a little shit. Do you know that?" His voice raised as his eyes teared up. "What do *you* have against me, huh?" He leaned over and jammed a bony finger into my sternum. "You're the one person in life who *should* love me, should even *like me,* dammit!"

He hurled his glass of wine into the fire, sending a cloud of grape hiss up the chimney. "Maybe that's the me in you, you little pissant. Next time you're touching yourself out in the woods looking for an imaginary ape, I want you to dwell on that." He stood up from the rocking chair and hobbled towards his room, snatching the bottle of merlot and an unopened sequel. "Shabbat shalom. Goodnight."

I could think of nothing to say. I listened to his door slam shut and thought I heard a cork pop. I realized that I'd gone over the edge and pushed him too far, but masked my embarrassment and shame under a banner of self-righteousness. I lied to myself, saying I told him what someone should have years ago, balling my fists and resolving to avoid an apology. *Let him drink it out*, I thought. *Actually, not a bad idea for myself.* I grabbed my car keys and abandoned the house, arriving at Former's and the exact same wine selection minutes later.

I reversed my decision after three glasses of wine. I had been in the wrong, I *had* been a little shit, and owed the old man an apology. I mentally rehearsed my speech as I parked my car again at his house. I would knock on his door and bring in two glasses of water so the hangover would not kill him the following day. I would qualify my apology with some kind of excuse, but by and large concede to him. Maybe even call Dad and exhort some sort of telephone reunion.

Before I got to the door I heard bleating from across the vineyard. I walked to the back corner of the house and looked out towards the Mexican quarters. A barely discernible goat stood hitched to the bunkhouse doorknob, near a couple of specks which might have been chickens. I turned around and saw the broken glass. The back door was shattered.

I ran to the Volvo and stuffed some of Cindy's silver-tipped bullets into my pocket. I threw open the front door and hit the lights. "Grampa!" I called. "Grampa, are you okay?"

No response. I felt a draft whip through the house. Breathing heavily, I fumbled for one of the rifles in the umbrella stand and loaded a silver bullet into it. I cocked the rifle and stalked through the living room and kitchen, searching for wolves. When I flipped on the kitchen light I saw one. Hulking and growling.

I fired. Missed.

The wolf lunged at me. I swung the gun down, cracking the butt of the rifle on the wolf's skull. I only dazed it; the angle had been too awkward to deliver much thrust. But it afforded me enough time to fumble for another bullet and reload the rifle. The wolf hustled past me, knocking over a stool. I fired a shot, blasting a hole through the microwave and spewing sparks across the kitchen.

I sprinted after the wolf, loading another bullet. It careened across the vineyard, dashing towards the safety of the woods. I took a careful bead on it and fired. A hit.

The wolf yelped and struggled to its feet. It limped towards the forest, painfully avoiding the use of its left hind leg. I squeezed off two more shots, but by then the distance and my nervous shaking made my accuracy moot. The wolf escaped.

"Grampa?" I said. I loaded the rifle in case there were any more surprises waiting for me in the house. "Grampa!" I yelled. "It's gone! Answer me!"

The door to his room was open. The light was still on.

The inside was littered with glass, shattered wine bottles and broken furniture. And blood. There was blood everywhere.

I found him lying in the corner. I dropped the

rifle and gasped.

    Grampa Rabbi was dead.

Chapter 17

"Isn't it horrible that a family can be torn apart by something as simple as a pack of wolves?"

—Jack Handey, *Deep Thoughts*

I later found out that mayor Greenely attended the funeral because the city council wanted a reliable witness to confirm Gunther Heinrich had actually died, and not just faking his own death for tax purposes.

Greenely pretended to be really worked up about the whole matter. He bear hugged me and Amos and my father, telling us how Nambersaw would never be the same again. He solemnly crept over to the casket and eased the lid open to get a peek. A moment later the wood snapped shut and the blood drained from his face. Amos put a meaty hand on his shoulder and pulled him back. "There's a reason we opted for closed casket, Mr. Mayor."

The attending Heinrichs showed nothing but dignity and poise throughout. Earlier at the Waffle House reception, when the assembled funeral-goers shook hands with us and dropped well-intended clichés, Amos smiled graciously and assured people that "Dad lived a long, full, and colorful life. How he died is awful, but I'm sure he'd prefer it over a boring passage like slipping away in his sleep." Of course, Amos was also very drunk, and probably assumed he was inheriting the vineyard. So it was easier for him to take things in stride.

My father said nothing. Which matched the general theme of the funeral: silence. No rabbi would dare attend, let alone preside, over the final sendoff of the Colonel Kurtz of Judaism. That would be tantamount to posthumously consecrating his hillbilly religion. There was no eulogy, no hymns. Just six Mexican pall-bearers trudging through snow before lowering a coffin into a pit. The only sound uttered was a single shotgun salute, fired off by an ancient but triumphant Harry Bradford.

My father is half Choctaw and his skin turns the color of an old penny during the summer. But on that winter morning he looked ashen. Neither depressed nor elated at the passing of his father. Just empty and confused. He exuded a harrowed dignity in his grief—back rigid, his eyes dry and distant and sad.

Cindy sat with me to fill up the otherwise scant front row. She does not fare well at funerals. She is a neon and pastel girl, violently reacting to black. She cried and squeezed my hand, though she met my grandfather only once. I felt her ring click against the one she had made me, which I wore for the first time that day. I squeezed hers back and tried to channel my own reticent tears, to weep vicariously through her. Eventually I would cry, I knew, but not in front of people. Not for a while.

Once everyone had a chance to ceremonially toss a clump of dirt on top of the coffin, I hugged Cindy and drifted towards the rented limousine. Which was, I think, jointly owned by the mortuary and town wedding chapel, because a hand-made sign on the back said "Just married!" and there were cans tied to the bumper. But none of us had ever ridden in a limousine before, so we didn't complain.

Dr. and Mrs. Rougarou stopped me before I climbed in. "Maurice, Cally," I said, befuddled. "I didn't know you were here. Thank you, you're very kind."

Mrs. Rougarou gave me a big hug, rocking back and forth. "You're family with us, okay Saul?" She blew into a hankie and smiled weakly.

Dr. Rougarou gave me a more respectable hug. "Our thoughts are with you, Saul."

"Thank you. Is Natalie here?" I hadn't expected any of them to turn up, but was hoping Natalie did.

"No, she's got the flu unfortunately," Maurice said. "I think I gave it to her, poor girl. Sometimes when you're the town doctor you're also the town petri dish, unfortunately. She'll be fine, but she's decommissioned for the next few days. Otherwise she would be here."

"She wanted to come," Cally said, "But we wouldn't let her. Nasty, nasty symptoms."

"Well, tell her to hang in there. I'll probably call her tonight."

"Sure, sure," said Maurice. "Well, listen, we were going to invite you to spend Christmas with us, but I can't in good conscience have guests over with such a crummy virus hanging around the house. If you'll call my office and give me your address, I'll drive your presents out here in the next couple of days."

"Oh, that's very nice," I said. "Thank you, I'll be sure to do that."

He squeezed my shoulder and gave a perfunctory smile. "Okay, you take care of yourself, Saul. We'll see you soon." He leaned in. "Saul," he whispered, "we'll get Phenris. We'll bring the wolves to justice."

I nodded, then climbed into the stretch limousine across from Amos and my stoic father. The car pulled forward and I watched my grandparents' tombstones roll away.

On the left, Gladys Black Kettle Heinrich. "Daughter, mother and beloved, beloved wife."

Next to it sprouted the fresh and polished tombstone of her reunited spouse: "Here interred lies Gunther Otis Heinrich. Vintner, citizen and sage. His loss is grieved by all mankind." Then in smaller letters at the bottom, as if an afterthought, read "Particularly by his good friend Ian Tabbum, proprietor of Tabbum's Tombstones, finest memorials in town at unbeatable prices. Rest in Peace."

Chapter 18

"Behold, I send you forth as sheep in the midst of wolves."

—The Gospel of Luke

The following day I resolved to kill Arno Phenris.

It seemed like a pretty cut-and-dry answer to me. He was 1. A murderer. 2. A werewolf, and 3. An asshole. Quite enough to justify putting him down. And if I did it while he was a wolf, there would be no time consuming first-degree murder trial. Animal cruelty at most, but probably not, given that whatever judge heard my case would know for a fact my own grandfather had been torn apart by "wild dogs" days earlier.

I think blood vengeance has been so wildly popular with mankind because it provides a productive outlet for feelings which otherwise lead to unpleasant mourning and reflection on impending mortality. Adrenaline is a more effective anti-depressant than Xanax, while also conducive to fresh air and the outdoors.

I loaded my backpack full of granola bars, bottled water and ammunition, stowing it on the floorboards of my passenger seat with a rifle. My plan to bring down Arno Phenris was not fully evolved, but I felt arming myself to the teeth somehow remedied an absence of careful preparation. I intended to drive out to Lycan and barricade myself inside the shed while it was still light out. The werewolves would probably smell me and come poking around. Then, I hoped, Arno would appear in the window to smirk and cajole me from the shed, at which point I would forcefully insert a silver bullet in his right nostril and listen to it zip around the inside of his skull. I didn't have much of an exit strategy worked out yet, but trusted I could come up with one on the fly.

I wanted to see Natalie first. I did not want the lights to go out on a boobless day, in the likely event that wolfmen succeeded in mauling me. I pulled up to her house after lunch. The Rougarou household had been decked out for Christmas, only two days away. Hundreds of bulbs studded the roof and a giant bell and bow-laden wreath hung from the door. Mrs. Rougarou greeted me. "Saul?" she asked, eyes wide. "What are you doing here?"

"Hi Mrs. Rougarou. I thought I'd go liven Natalie's spirits."

"Well, that's very nice Saul, but she's quite ill. Just say hello and go home." I gave her uncharacteristically terse statement a quizzical expression. Her mouth formed a straight line as she gathered her thoughts. "It's dangerous for you to be here, Saul. What with Arno gone crazy. I want you to leave." Then her eyes softened. "I'll make you a sandwich for the ride home."

"Okay," I said. "Don't worry about me picking anything up from Nat, I have a terrific immune system. And I'll leave soon enough."

"Before dark, I want her resting."

"Yes ma'am."

221

"Okay," she said slowly. "She's in her room."

The inside of the house was a Christmas card. Garlands and stockings draped over the fireplace mantle. A real pine tree dominated the living room, overshadowing a collection of immaculate, shining presents. Ornamental nutcrackers dotted the home like wooden sentries. I weaved through the holiday decorations up the stairs to Natalie's room. She laid in bed curled up with a novel. "Hey," I said. "Feeling any better?"

She sat up and smiled weakly. "Yeah, a little. I'm so glad you're here! Thanks for coming over."

"My pleasure." I crawled underneath the sheets and felt her body heat greet me like a warm bath. "You know what's best for the flu," I said. "Getting—"

Mrs. Rougarou opened the door. "Saul?" She stood in the doorway. "It's very nice of you to visit Natalie, but she's going to bed early tonight. Aren't you, Nat?" Her daughter nodded. "I'll ask you to leave here shortly. Maurice will come up to get you when he gets home from work."

"Sure, okay," I said. Which was the plan anyway. I wanted a daylight advantage in fortifying the shed for another lycanthrope siege.

"Hands test," Mrs. Rougarou announced. I wasn't sure what she was talking about until Natalie held both fists above her head and nudged me with an elbow. Ah, to make sure we weren't giving each other hand jobs. I held my fists aloft as well. "Just checking. Okay, you two take it easy."

"You're in luck," I said after Mrs. Rougarou descended the stairs. "As you have contracted the flu, I'm not even trying to get you aroused. My only ambition is to cuddle." (I was lying.)

"Mmmm," she said, curling up and pressing her back to my chest.

We lay there for a few minutes, her nodding off and me thinking about where to prop up my rifle when I got to the shed. My right arm fell asleep so I pulled it out from under her and slid it under her neck, holding her hand in mine. Two seconds passed and she jerked it away. "Ow!" she said. "Did you just pinch me?"

"No. You must have been dreaming."

"Okay, sorry," she mumbled. She reached out for my hand, then pulled it back. "Stop!"

I pulled back, unsure of what she was talking about. "I'm just holding your hand."

"Do you have a buzzer or a lighter or something?"

"No." I observed my palms for confirmation. "Only this ring Cindy made me." I stopped. I peered at the ring. The silver ring.

Natalie started to shake. Slowly, I began to pull the covers down. "Saul," she said, her voice quivering. "Remember the werewolf of St. Almo?" She inhaled sharply. I pulled the sheet away. A large white bandage covered her thigh. "One year his wife opened the door on Christmas, or forgot to lock it, or something. And he killed her." I stared at the bandage, my ring, and the bandage. "They found him at the edge of town, covered in blood. They were going to kill him, but he hanged himself first."

I pulled my neck up to look into her face. Tears were streaming down her cheeks. She was trembling. "It was you?" I asked. "*You!?*"

A river of tears drenched her pillow. "No!" she

cried, shaking her head back and forth frantically. "It's not me! Saul! I love you! I'm so sorry!" She tried to cup my face with her hands but I pulled away. "I'm not like that, Saul! I wish it wasn't me! I'm so sorry! Please! I didn't mean to." I scrambled out of her bed. She groped after me, clutching my pant leg. "I can't *help* it, Saul! I love you!"

I stood in the middle of her room, chest heaving, fists clenched. My nostrils flared. My blood boiled. "You're all a bunch of damned werewolves, aren't you?" She nodded, weeping and shivering. I glared at her. "You're not Little Red Riding Hood. You're the wolf." I stormed out of her room, slamming the door shut behind me. Natalie wailed as I ran down the stairs.

Mrs. Rougarou stood up. "Saul? It's getting late, you need to head home now."

"You're damned right I do!" I kicked a lamp over and threw the front door open, banging it against the wall. Mrs. Rougarou chased after me as I dashed towards my car.

"Saul!" she yelled. "Solomon Heinrich! You know?" Her voice trembled in fear, in anger. "So you know now?"

I glared at her. "Yes I do! I know that you're *all* a bunch of monsters! Even your murdering bitch of a daughter!"

Her jaw clenched and her eyes narrowed. "Then you know how dangerous it is for you to be here, tonight. It's the Solstice. Most any other time of year we can hold back. We *do* hold back. But not now, not this week. Do you understand?"

"Yes," I said, opening the door to my Volvo.

"*Do you?*" she screamed. "Because as soon as the

moon comes up you're going to be in a whole town of 'monsters!' Surrounded by a forest of 'monsters!' Do you understand that?"

I grabbed the rifle from under my seat and held it up. "That's what I'm counting on, Mrs. Rougarou." I cocked the gun and climbed into the car. "I'd stay in tonight if I were you."

Chapter 19

"The beast in me is caged by frail and fragile bars."

—Johnny Cash

It's pretty hard to operate a rifle while simultaneously driving a car, but if you're pissed off enough and don't mind running people over you can probably do it too.

Such is the state of mind I found myself in as dusk settled. Driving in circles through the town, my gun poking out the window. Denizens stared at me, agape. Mine was the only car on the road. All other people were on foot. Sitting outside in lawn chairs, idling on cul de sacs, exiting their homes. Waiting for the moon.

The more I drove, the angrier I became. Natalie was a murderer. Her parents were liars. The town they lived in was a farce with window boxes. What I had taken to be good and decent was treacherous and evil. Lycan might be a Norman Rockwell painting, but it was his portrait of Dorian Gray.

I slammed on the brakes as a man rushed my car. Maurice stood in the middle of the road, arms outstretched and scrambling. His white lab coat fluttered behind him like a cape.

I honked. "Get the fuck outta my way!"

"Saul!" he yelled. He dashed to the passenger door and flung it open.

"Go home, Maurice." I inched the car forward.

"Find a good chew toy and take a night off."

He jumped into the moving Volvo. "Saul," he panted, his eyes gigantic. "What on earth are you doing?"

I pulled the gun from the window and laid it across my lap, angling it towards his love handles. "I'm hunting, Maurice. Hunting werewolves." I turned a corner and glanced at him. "Seen any?" He said nothing. Townfolk stared quizzically at us as we drove by, some of them noticeably agitated. Congregating in front of their gingerbread homes in Christmas sweaters and wool hats. We drove past a family unpacking an ice chest of raw beef and lamb.

"Saul," he said slowly, "you don't know what's going on here. Get out of town. Now. Before the moon is up."

I shook my head and flipped the lights on. Sunset.

"No good, Doc. My girlfriend killed my grandfather." I slammed the brakes, turning to face Maurice. "*Because she's a werewolf!*" He thumped into the dashboard with an *oomph*. I eased my foot off the pedal and sighed. "That shit's not in the Boy Scout manual, Maurice."

He grimaced and flexed both hands. His jaw popped loudly as he opened and closed his mouth. "That was terrible, Saul. We're all heartbroken over Gunther's death, *especially* Natalie. But you have to understand that she wasn't in control of herself. None of us can when we're lupine. Arno and the pack can, but they spend their lives that way. When we transform, we go mad. Territorial and crazed. Natalie loves you. She never meant to hurt anyone."

"Oh, okay," I said. "Be sure to thank her for not

227

showing up to his funeral. That would have been awkward in retrospect."

He remained as calm as a man with a rifle nuzzling his belly button lint can. "I know you're upset Saul. And scared."

"Mostly just pissed off," I said. "But that's nothing a warm gun can't fix."

"You *should* be scared," he continued. "Because this entire town is minutes from transforming."

"Into bloodthirsty werewolves?"

"Bloodthirsty," he said, pondering the word. He looked out the window. An older couple in scarves and ear muffs watched us cruise by from deck chairs. One waved a mitten. "Do you honestly think we enjoy becoming wolves?"

"Arno Phenris seems to get a kick out of it."

"Arno *is* a wolf. We're skinwalkers." I harrumphed. "What I originally told you about Lycan was correct, but only half the story. Everybody here has lycanthropy. Everyone. The Wichitas had it, the Creoles who joined them had it, too. For—" he leaned forward and grimaced, clenching his fists.

"Easy now," I said, nudging him with the gun.

He wiped a bead of sweat from his forehead. "For years Lycan was a rallying point for werewolves. My grandfather came over from France. The Bisclavrets are an ancient family from Brittany. Over time, though, some people decided they didn't like being human. They moved into the woods. Werewolves." He raked fingernails back and forth across his abdomen.

"The rest saw themselves as men, and remained in Lycan. Learned how to suppress the condition as much as possible. The wolves call us 'skinwalkers.'

And just as you see a werewolf as a freak, they see us as monstrosities. Wolves who parade around as people." He took a deep breath, exhaling it with a noticeable shudder. "Although Lowell's death escalated the recent tensions between us, it didn't start them. For years they've insisted we're living a lie, that we're cavorting in flesh suits. That we should give up our farms and homes and return to the forest."

"But you see yourselves as men?" I asked, my words pregnant with sarcasm. "Just regular blokes?"

"Men afflicted by a terrible disease. That necessitates secrecy from the outside world." His cheeks were dark with Nixonesque five o'clock shadow. "We only transform for one week. Not bad," he said, arching his eyebrows. "It used to be a lot worse. Back before the pill."

"What?" I asked, looking at him through slitted eyes. "What on earth are you babbling about?"

"Men are only affected during the solstice. We've learned to suppress the condition the rest of the year. Women, though. . ."

"What?"

"Well, what does the moon regulate, Saul?"

"Tides."

"And?" He coughed. Groaned.

"Werewolves."

"Yes," he nodded. "But why would the moon set off the syndrome in anyone?"

"I don't know."

"If not for artificial lighting, it would set the pace for menstrual cycles. Which trigger lycanthropy in women."

"Wait. . ." I said. This was *almost* funny. "Do you

229

mean that. . . that when women here have PMS they turn into werewolves?" He nodded. "That's where the whole full moon thing comes from? Werewolf PMS?"

For a split second, we nearly laughed. Thinking the same chauvinistic joke. Which made me feel particularly bad about keeping the loaded gun against his gut.

"Girls take birth control as soon as safely possible to avert the syndrome. So we all suppress the urge, but we can't hold it forever. It's the worst during the solstice, and that's when we let go. For a week, every night, we give in. Turn into wolves."

I clenched my jaw. "Why didn't you *tell* me this, Maurice?"

He frowned, his brow sweaty and crumpled. He looked constipated. "These are my people," he whispered, his voice turning throaty and horse. "I had to protect them. Protect our secret." He winced and leaned over, placing a hand over mine on top of the steering wheel. "Please," he growled. "Go. Away."

I turned to face him. The skin on his face was taught, stretched like rubber over increasingly angular features. His mustache had cartoonishly sprouted into a full handlebar, groping towards unkempt sideburns. His breaths were short and heavy, his teeth sharp and large.

The eyes remained the same. Kind, frightened, pleading. I stopped the car. "Get out, Maurice." I leaned over to open the door. "Go home."

He opened his mouth to speak but failed to do so. He toppled out of the car and landed on all fours, scurrying across a lawn. His head bowed and his back arched as hair burst from every pore. In the fresh darkness of night it looked like he was spontaneously bleeding ink.

So did the rest of the town.

Chapter 20

"Wolves are very resourceful. All they need to survive is for people not to shoot them."

—Bob Ferris

The moon rose above the horizon, a swollen pale-faced cantaloupe of evil. The air filled with an electric tension as people rose from their lawn chairs to peer at the sinister orb.

They began to scream. Tearing their cardigans and mufflers off. Doubling over and sprouting hair. Thrashing, growing fangs, falling onto the manicured lawns and contorting into weird shapes. I have never been so frightened in my entire life. Even the night in the shed felt less terrifying than watching a whole village of humans devolve into snarling beasts.

A man bolted out of his house and onto the street, yelling and waving his hands. His shirt was half off, his face lupine and frothing. I swerved to the right but he ran at me, snarling and slicing his hands through the air. He collided with the Volvo, launching the car into a spin.

I hit the brakes and gripped the wheel, panting. My vision blurred momentarily from the shock. When it normalized, the landscape around me looked even more horrifying. Little evidence of humanity remained in the town. Wolves were running in and out of open doors, pissing on fire hydrants, rooting through overturned dumpsters, humping on lawns. A *lot* of humping on lawns.

A wolf jumped up the side of my car and lunged for me, narrowly missing my face with its teeth. I screamed and leaned over to avoid the snapping jaws. I jammed my foot on the gas and launched the car forward, but the wolf managed to lodge itself in the window, hanging out the side of the car. I sped up but it hung on, struggling to climb all the way in. It growled and snapped at me, clawing at my left arm. I released the steering wheel and grabbed my rifle. Fired.

The blast knocked the wolf clear from the car, spraying blood across the windshield. I lunged for the steering wheel, but too late. The Volvo careened over a curb, plowing through a wolf in the process. I jerked the wheel to the right and angled towards the road, then instinctively ducked as I obliterated a trashcan, spilling its contents across the hood. The car shot off the curb and skidded on asphalt. I spun the wheel to the left, struggling to keep it from jumping the opposite curb.

I regained control of the car just in time to clip a telephone pole.

The Volvo spun sickeningly, partially wrapping around the splintered wood. The windshield shattered and the seatbelt tore into my shoulder. I moaned and wiped glass out of my hair. Blood spurted from my nose, although I did not think I'd personally slammed into anything. My neck felt like someone had smacked it with a baseball bat.

I tried to reverse the car but it refused. The engine made a final desperate clicking noise and fell silent. Horrified, I leaned over and fumbled with the box of silver-tipped ammunition. I stuffed fistfuls of bullets into my pockets and grabbed the rifle. My door jammed, but I managed to elbow it open and stagger into the street.

I wiped the blood from my nose and frantically looked around. There was a parked Buick nearby, but it turned out to be locked and with no keys in the ignition. I darted my head in every direction, searching for a bicycle, another car, anything. Six wolves turned a corner and bounded towards me. I screamed, panicking and looking for a place to hide.

I ran to the nearest house and wrenched the door knob. Locked. I propped my rifle against the door and grabbed a trash can, hurling it through the front window. My shin sliced open as I stepped over the shattered glass. I flipped the lights on and searched for car keys. I hoped to find a basement I could barricade myself inside until morning.

A wolf crashed through the back window and picked itself up. The hackles on its spine raised and its face, torn from glass shards, snarled at me.

"Back!" I screamed. It leaned into a pouncing position, preparing to jump, and I shot. Wolves poured through the broken window, prompting me to fling the back door open and run out onto the patio.

I spotted a tree house in the yard. I slammed the door shut behind me and bolted towards the fort, hearing glass shatter. I darted up the wooden planks fastened to the base of the tree. Wolves collected underneath it, clawing and jumping on the bark, hoping to snag a pants leg.

I grabbed the next plank and nearly fell over as the rotten wood came apart in my hand.

Repositioning my feet, I stretched to grab the next board up, lurching backwards as it came lose. Below me, the wolves howled. I could feel the plank I stood on wobble.

"Go away!" I yelled, aiming my rifle at the monsters. "Get! I'll shoot!" They growled in response.

I looked around. There was no way to get to the platform on top, if its boards could support my weight anyway. But there *was* a limb extending towards the house. If I could swing on top of it I might be able to work my way towards the roof and reach for the gutter.

I tucked the rifle under my arm and reached out to grab the limb with my right hand. The board I stood on creaked and popped out of the trunk. I managed to grab the limb with both hands just as my footing gave way.

The rifle clattered to the ground with a thud. "Fuck!" I said. "Just. . . just *fuck!*" One of the wolves lifted a leg to squirt urine on it.

I worked my way down the limb, hand-over-hand, inching towards the house. The wood creaked. It started to dip as I maneuvered away from the trunk. The wolves made running lunges at me, barely missing my shoes with their teeth.

But I was near the house. The roof was a foot away, but also a few feet below me. I might just be able to drop to it.

Not worth the risk, I decided. I released my left hand and prepared to turn around, hoping to retrace my steps to the tree fort. Maybe I could swing up at the base of the limb and straddle it until daylight.

It cracked.

I lurched downward, almost losing my grip on the bark. The wolves whined and formed a hungry circle beneath me. "Dammit," I said, nearly crying. Taking a deep breath, I swung back and forth, letting go of the branch moments before it snapped loose of the tree. I grabbed the gutter with my fingers and held on for dear life. I gripped the gutter with every muscle in my body, and pounded my feet against the wall, desperately trying to propel myself up onto the roof.

I managed to clamber up, straining and sweating. I collapsed against the slanted roof and heaved giant, terrified breaths that billowed out as clouds in the cool air. The wolves howled in anguish below. By now I really regretted sticking around Lycan past dark. Seeing a whole town turn into bloodthirsty werewolves will do that to you, particularly if you're not a very good marksman.

"You bastards!" I shouted. I turned around and squatted on the edge, still gasping for air. "Shut up!" They didn't. "Go to hell!" I dug a hand into my pocket and withdrew a fistful of impotent bullets. I hurled them down at the wolves. The hail of metal projectiles elicited yelps, but that was it. The wolves were further agitated, though I felt slightly better.

I sighed and felt my adrenaline begin to lessen. I was safe. For the moment, anyway. There was no way wolves were going to get on the roof.

A gust of wind blew down my collar and I shivered. I was in for a cold, cold night. It occurred to me that perching on the edge was not a long-term option. I could lie down, but only by jamming my feet into the gutters. If I sat, dangling my legs off the edge, I risked slipping on the slick surface.

I look walked over to a procession of plastic reindeer and a Santa to find a better resting point. By straddling my legs around the peak and putting my back to the chimney, I could find a reasonably comfortable position to enjoy hypothermia in. Then climb down the following day and hope the werewolves were sleeping, or at least exhausted when returned to human form.

I carefully climbed up the side, once losing my footing in the process and nearly tumbling down to the wolves below. But I managed to get to the peak.

Right before I lost my footing again.

I pitched forward over the peak and slid down the opposite side of the roof, blindly clawing and grabbing at the tiles whooshing by. I could gain no traction against the frosty surface. With a dizzying silence, I slid off the edge, did half a flip in mid-air, and landed flush on my back with a painful thud.

I lay in the grass, disoriented and in tremendous pain. *Perhaps I will just go to sleep*, I thought. *"A" for effort.*

But then my will to survive, which had taken longer to fall off the edge than I did, plopped down into me and I sat up. I felt myself and checked for broken bones. Maybe a busted rib, but my legs were okay. Just a whole lot of bruises and scrapes. I stood up and suppressed the urge to moan.

I needed a backup plan. *Okay, just try and hide in the house. Creep back in through the broken window and shut yourself in a closet. Hope that they did not hear or smell you and wait in terrified darkness until morning comes, then hobble away to safety.*

I limped towards the front door and stopped. The garage door was agape. Inside it I could see a

Ford Taurus and a golf cart reflecting moonlight. *A golf cart!*

I hobbled over to it and inspected the vehicle. "Yamaha Turbo Cart" gleamed in inset text on its dashboard. The speedometer extended all the way to thirty-five miles an hour. They keys were in the ignition.

I lowered myself into the seat and took a deep breath. Okay. This was it. I turned the ignition on and the golf cart purred. "Oh," I said, approaching tears, "*thank* you." The cart skidded off the driveway, nearly flipping over, and sputtered down the street.

Behind me the wolves crooned with ecstatic fury. They bounded after the cart with locomotive resolve. My foot jammed against the gas and pumped it back and forth, pleading with the Yamaha to exceed my expectations for it.

It accelerated at a steady but maddeningly patient speed. The wolves were gaining. Ten of them now. Howling and tearing down the street, a pack of death gone berserk. I reached behind me and tipped a bag of golf clubs over, spilling them onto the asphalt and tripping a couple of my pursuers.

For the next five minutes I careened through a Tiger Woods nightmare, whizzing away from a pack of wolves on a sputtering golf cart. I kept gaining distance on the level road, but for every foot acquired between myself and my pursuers, another wolf joined the pack. The cart's engine sounded an intruder alarm to the entire community.

The town hemorrhaged fur. As I sped through Lycan wolves poured towards me from every direction, jumping hedges, bursting from dog doors, scattering pink flamingos. Every house sported extravagant Christmas lights, casting shadows of the beasts across lawns. I glanced in the rear view mirror and could see nothing but frenzied, muscular bodies bounding after the golf cart, illumined by the soft glow of holiday displays. I reached up to brake the rear view mirror off in my hand, then turned around and chucked it at the pack.

I nearly pissed myself. There were hundreds of them. Maybe a thousand, whatever Lycan's population was, all united in a Brothers Grimm hunting expedition. A marathon of flashing teeth and hungry eyes. A quarter of a mile behind me.

I took a deep breath and gripped the wheel until my knuckles turned white. *Okay*, I thought, *The point is that you're gaining ground. Ten more minutes and you'll be out of sight.* I passed a white house, Lycan's final outpost, and whizzed beside a pasture towards the forest.

The engine sputtered and the speed dipped. "C'mon, c'mon," I pleaded.

A tiny red light caught my eye. A little LED light no bigger than a marble, but its crimson glow painted terror across my face. The fuel gage. I scanned the horizon frantically for anything. I turned back to look behind me. The house I had passed was still closer than the forest, but the wolves were in hot pursuit. If I could get to the house, then somehow climb its roof. . .

I swung the golf cart to the right, skidding on two wheels. For one terrible moment I thought it would capsize, but it righted and whizzed towards the tiny homestead.

Now I was driving directly towards the pack, racing them to my only possible sanctuary. The golf cart slowed and died, inching on the asphalt by virtue of inertia and fervent hope. I hopped off as it rolled to a stop and sprinted towards the house, inadvertently plunging my foot into a pothole. My hands and knees lit ablaze as I tripped into frost and asphalt. I stood up and lurched forward but toppled in pain. My ankle was sprained. I limped towards the house, dragging the swollen joint.

After a few steps I sat down on the pavement and took a deep sigh. I wasn't going to make it. I could hear the wolves snapping their jaws open and shut in anticipation. They would beat me to the house. Devour me. Wolves would maul wolves, just trying to get a taste of my blood.

I fell backwards and laid on my back. I imagine humans are the only animals capable of admitting defeat. We're the only ones smart enough to truly comprehend inevitable demise. I exhaled a quivering breath and stared up at the moon. Directly above me, shining over the night like an ivory button.

"Señor Heinrich!"

I sat up. A pickup skidded to a halt. Miguel jumped frantically in the back. "Señor Heinrich!" he repeated. "Vamos! Vamos!"

Shocked, I limped towards the truck as the sounds of homicidal panting closed in. Miguel leaned forward and grabbed my wrists, just as the first incisors sank into my shoes and pants.

The truck shot forward. I screamed as my knees skidded across the asphalt, but the pack lost its grip. Miguel wrenched me into the truck bed and I collapsed on the metal floorboard, bleeding and gasping for air. Pedro and two others sat inside the cab.

Miguel staggered off balance for a moment before dropping against the rear view window with a thump. His jaw dropped in terror as he watched the throng of monsters chasing after us.

A wolf, elastic underwear stretched around its rear, howled and charged the bumper. I spotted a handful of werewolves who had not fully transformed. A frightening posse of half-men screaming and loping after us.

Miguel cocked a rifle and aimed it at the underwear-clad wolf. "Stop," I said, lifting up on the shaft. He pulled the trigger and fired harmlessly into the air.

"Los lobos!" he screamed, infuriated at me for the misfire. He aimed again.

"No!" I smacked the gun away. "Leave them alone. Let's just get the hell out of here. They won't be able to give chase for long."

Glaring at me, he put the rifle on safety and crossed it over his lap.

I pulled myself up and sat against the rear window with Miguel, watching the throng of death receding into the distance. "Thank you for rescuing me," I said. "Muchas gracias."

Miguel nervously watched the pack of wolves. "De nada."

"How did you know to come get me?"

He turned to face me before resuming his sentinel gaze over the asphalt. "Su abuelo."

"My grandfather?" I asked, confused. "My grandfather is dead."

He looked at me grimly. "That is what *I* tell *him*."

Inside the truck, Pedro turned the radio to "Feliz

Navidad."

When we got back to Grampa's house I invited my Mexicans saviors to leave the stable house and move in with me. They declined. The bunkhouse afforded all their plastic saints and garlic strands and Virgin Mary merchandise.

As I lay in bed that night within my derelict inheritance, door barricaded shut with a dresser and a revolver under my pillow, I heard a wolf howl outside. I crept to the window to look at it. It stared up at me from the snow, sleek and gray. It loomed there for several moments before its ears flattened and it lifted its head to bay at the moon.

Long and sad, like the last voice on the planet.

When the howl concluded it turned and limped away. Wounded on her left hind leg.

Epilogue

"Last night I dreamed I was chasing a pack of wolves, trying to belong."

—Edgar Cayce

I no longer have the newspaper from the day after, but I recall the story featured on the third page of *The Nambersaw Minuteman*. It quietly mentioned that a head-on collision claimed the lives of three Lycan residents and injured a fourth. Phil Mentot, Pete Bourgot and Ralph Bisclavret. Ralph Bisclavret, the town milkman. Officially dead on impact from a car accident. "The involved families," the paper noted, "have requested prayers and privacy as they are left to grieve over the loss of their loved ones."

Nearly a decade has passed since that news blippet neatly glossed over the details of Lycan's carnage. Most of it uninteresting. I fled to Austin and got myself an office job, but then got fired and opened a microbrewery. I acquired a lease, a roommate and a tropical aquarium. My microbrewery failed and I got another office job. An article I wrote about Bigfoot helped purchase an entire season of *Frasier*.

I've returned to Lycan only once. Last Valentine's Day, when I spontaneously sped off in my car, hopped up on romantic comedies and desperate to find Natalie.

I visited the farm house, now under the joint

management of Amos and his silent partner Miguel, where my kith and kin gave me a hardy dinner. I drove through the Kiamichi Mountains towards Lycan, drumming my hands on the steering wheel, unsure if I would be shot or mauled on sight the moment I stepped into the eldritch town. Just before entering Lycan's city limits I parked the car and debated whether or not to give up on the madcap expedition and go back to the vineyard, and safety.

After a few deep breaths I gunned the ignition and backed the car up. And hit something. A soft *clunk* sounded off of my bumper.

"Oh God," I said. "Not again." I pulled a revolver out of my glove compartment and exited the car to investigate.

And I *swear*, standing behind the car, rubbing his knee, stood Bigfoot.

I gaped at him. He loomed eight feel tall, covered in fur, with an eerily human-like face. He said nothing. Then, with gargantuan strength, he pried the bumper off of my car and slung it under his arm like a snowboard. He walked back to the edge of the forest in a colossal stride, then paused. His eyes narrowed and he snorted, flipping his head back. The gesture trascended the species barrier, deftly communicating, "Go fuck yourself." He shoved the bumper my direction and shook it. As if to say, "See this? I keep it! I keep it!" Then he disappeared into the woods.

I stared after him for a full five minutes. Then I shrugged, got back into the car, and drove to Lycan. To find Natalie.

She was gone, of course. But so was everyone else.

They left behind a ghost town. Amos tells me that when Lycan folded up, subdivision developers swooped in to scavenge real estate deals. They offered contracts and plans to create a brand new suburbia. Level the old houses and replace them with a confederation of gated communities radiating out from a central Wal-Mart.

The denizens turned it down. They decided they would rather walk away with worthless deeds than see their childhoods suffocate beneath laminated spec homes and parking lots. Their town remains but is unpopulated. An abandoned hamlet of knee-high lawns, rust and boarded windows.

Amos isn't sure where they went. My guess is that most folks gave up on life as homo sapiens and drifted into the forest. Wolves now, occasionally tip-toeing back to Lycan to pick through the ruins, wondering if the coffee and school plays were all just a dream. Skinwalker holdouts must have scattered and relocated in search of anonymity and happiness elsewhere. I wish them the best.

Last night a harvest moon hovered above the Austin skyline. I gazed up at that luminous softball and wondered if, far away, intelligent howls were rising to the same orb. Former accountants, waitresses and firemen, now stalking boars in the Quachitas. I thought about the Rougarous and the hand I played in unwittingly decimating their town. A milkman hangs from my neck like an albatross.

I feel that there is some grand lesson I should deduce from the experience, but damned if I know what it is. "Enjoy life when it's happy, because sooner or later werewolves drop in and screw everything up." What? Nobody's putting *that* in a fortune cookie. Or, "Better to lose a lover than love a monster"? Warmer, I guess. We're up to the eloquence of bathroom graffiti. I suppose if Natalie had been less assiduous with condoms I would have contracted lycanthropy, then made a career giving Safe Sex talks at Oklahoma public schools.

A postcard arrived for me in the mail last week. On one side is a picture of a dairy cow with a bell around its neck, dumbly gazing at the hulking mountains behind it. "Beautiful Nidau, Switzerland!" it boasts. No name on the reverse, no return address. Only flowing, feminine cursive:

We miss you. I miss you. Come home, Saul.

I keep it in my desk drawer at work. I must look at the damn thing twenty times a day. On occasion I smell it. My co-workers probably think I have dirty pictures next to my paper clips or something.

This morning I gave my boss my two weeks notice. He stared at it like I'd handed him a conk shell. "You're leaving? Why?"

I smiled and shook my head, returning to my desk.

"Because I think I could be happy as a werewolf."

Acknowledgements

Thank you Audrey Dodgen, who took time away from being a stellar photographer to proofread my book.

A special thanks also to J. M. Jennings and Andrew Young for their creative input. Both are brilliant men and good friends.

Mr. Jennings is a powerful writer, who continues to offer equal parts moral support and keen insight.

Andrew Young has a peculiar habit of reading my manuscripts, entirely forgetting to tell me he has, then contacting me months later with several hours of immeasurably helpful observations. I would have it no other way.

76408175R00143

Made in the USA
Columbia, SC
25 September 2019